Mademoiselle Colombe

A Play in Two Acts

by
Jean Anouilh

Adapted by
Louis Kronenberger

A SAMUEL FRENCH ACTING EDITION

SAMUEL FRENCH

FOUNDED 1830

SAMUELFRENCH.COM

MADEMOISELLE COLOMBE

STORY OF THE PLAY

Colombe is a little flower girl who meets a moody pianist backstage at a theatre. They are married. On the surface they are happy. When he is drafted into the army, his actress mother, a temperamental darling of the Parisian stage, gives Colombe a part in her play.

When the puritanical pianist comes home on a brief leave of absence, he learns that Colombe has been unfaithful. Even with his own brother. When he confronts her with her infidelity, she is unabashed. His dour way has not been to her liking. She is happy in her bohemian life.

As for the mother, she has eight husbands herself. She has married for money and position. Love and marriage she tells him are temporary things. His heart is broken? Then mend it, but don't torment others with his trouble. People have too many of their own, which they hide better than he does.

Program of first performance of *Mademoiselle Colombe* as produced at the Longacre Theatre, January 6, 1954.

ROBERT L. JOSEPH and JAY JULIEN

Present

JULIE HARRIS
EDNA BEST

in

MADEMOISELLE COLOMBE

A play by Jean Anouilh

Adapted by Louis Kronenberger with
Eli Wallach
Sam Jaffe
Harry Bannister, Mikhail Rasumny, Frank Silvera, and
William Windom

Directed by Harold Clurman

Production designed by Boris Aronson

Costumes by Motley

Production associate, Shirley Bernstein

CAST

(In order of appearance)

COLOMBE	*Julie Harris*
JULIEN	*Eli Wallach*
MME. GEORGES	*Edna Preston*
MME. ALEXANDRA	*Edna Best*
CHIROPODIST	*Edward Julien*
MANICURIST	*Joanne Taylor*
HAIRDRESSER	*Nehemiah Persoff*
GOURETTE	*Sam Jaffe*

4

EDOUARD .... *William Windom*
DESCHAMPS .... *Frank Silvera*
POET-MINE-OWN .... *Mikhail Rasumny*
GAULOIS .... *Harry Bannister*
DANCERS .... *{Lee Philips*
{Jeanne Jerrems
STAGEHAND .... *Gregory Robins*

The action takes place in a Paris theatre around 1900.

ACT I

SCENE 1 : *A backstage corridor and Mme. Alexandra's dressing-room.*

SCENE 2 : *The stage. A few days later.*

ACT II

SCENE 1 : *A corridor and Colombe's dressing-room. Three months later.*

SCENE 2 : *The stage. Three hours later.*

EPILOGUE : *The stage. Two years earlier.*

(The Curtain will not be lowered between Scene 2 and the Epilogue)

Mademoiselle Colombe

ACT ONE

Scene I

(CORRIDOR LIGHTS up. DRESSING ROOM LIGHTS dim.)

Scene: *The corridor flanking the dressing rooms. The corridor runs from up Right to down Right. The main entrance up Right and two steps down leads to the stage. At Right two steps down lead to a dressing room. At Left is the door to Mme. Alexandra's dressing room: the whole side and front of this room is exposed. A door Left opens into her inner dressing room, off Left. Inside the main dressing room, Left of Center, are a large ornate canopied dressing-table and mirror. Right of table, a throne-like armchair and footstool. Left above door, another armchair. Down Left a cheval mirror on a stand. Down Right two fancy poufs. Up Right of Center an elaborate screen. Behind the screen, a small table and chair. Baskets of flowers distributed round the room; also a large Persian rug, and two small animal skins.*

At Rise: Colombe *is in the corridor seated in a chair down Right and* Julien *pacing back and forth. They seem to be waiting for something The dresser,* Mme. Georges, *comes in from dressing room off Right carrying a stool.*

6

MME. GEORGES. *(Placing stool down Left of corridor)* Sit down, Mr. Julien. You'll probably have to wait a while.

JULIEN. *(At some distance)* Thanks, Georgïe—but I just told you I'd rather stand.

MME. GEORGES. My oldest boy had to stand, too. Now he's got varicose veins. I always have to sit and it's just the opposite—my rear end hurts.

JULIEN. Oh, go bury your rear end. I wish the old girl would hurry up.

MME. GEORGES. *(To* COLOMBE*)* Thirty years I've been a dresser, Madame Julien, always sitting around waiting for the play to end.

COLOMBE. But you don't *have* to sit.

MME. GEORGES. Yes I do. My phlebetis.

JULIEN. The hell with your phlebetis. Find out if the old girl's on stage.

MME. GEORGES. *(Shaking her head)* Uh uhm. She always goes to her dressing room before she rehearses. —A fine way to refer to your mother.

JULIEN. Stop lecturing me.

MME. GEORGES. Listen to him. My oldest all over again. I will say, my third one, who died of T.B., was easy to bring up—always spitting quietly in his corner. *(To* COLOMBE*)* How old is *your* baby?

COLOMBE. Just a year.

MME. GEORGES. Are his movements regular?

JULIEN. *(Grabbing her in exasperation by the arm)* Georgie, if you don't shut up, I'll break your neck.

MME. GEORGES. *(Quite unruffled)* Men, Madame Julien— I've known him since he was so high.

JULIEN. Uhm. That's how long I've been hearing all this.

MME. GEORGES. He was a nice little boy. Always asked for caramels. Didn't you?

JULIEN. *(Letting her go and walking off to Right)* If you say so.

MME. GEORGES. *(To* JULIEN*)* *You* didn't have strong lungs either.

JULIEN. They're much stronger now. The caramels cured me.

MME. GEORGES. *(Sudden thought)* I hope the baby doesn't cough?

JULIEN. Georgie, my son doesn't cough, my wife doesn't cough, *(Indicating himself)* none of us cough. You *sure* they're rehearsing today? I've got to see her.

MME. GEORGES. Gets married without a word, waits two years, and then calmly strolls in just before a rehearsal. *(To* JULIEN) Don't worry, you'll see her—and hear from her, too. You and your mother have never gotten along. Not like your brother, Edouard: he knows how to handle her.

JULIEN. What's she playing in now?

MME. GEORGES. "The Goddess of Love." A play with five changes. Why can't she do "Athalie" again—a classic, and she only has to change once.

JULIEN. *(Taking her arm and urging her out)* Georgie, it's damn near three o'clock. Be a good girl, go down and see.

MME. GEORGES. *(Exiting as though her aches and pains were pieces of heavy luggage)* Two flights of stairs: have you any idea how many times I go up and down every day? *(Exits up Right of the corridor.)*

JULIEN. "The Goddess of Love." One of her *femme fatale* roles. That's bad.

COLOMBE. Why?

JULIEN. The only times I've made even a dent on her was when she was cast as a mother. The theatre's sure something!

COLOMBE. You make too much of everything.

JULIEN. Do I? *(Eruptively)* When I was four, my mother sent me to live with a blacksmith outside Paris. For months she never came near me. Just as I was half-dead from cold and hunger, Poet-Mine-Own brought her the script of "The Sins Of The Mother." In the first act she abandons her baby on the steps of a church—snowing outside, singing within. In the fifth act she's stabbed with remorse for ninety-one lines.

(Sitting on stool down Left) I once counted them— After the dress rehearsal, she got into a carriage with some friends and a photographer to see the poor little kid. Imagine the publicity! Madame Alexandra, the nation's greatest emotional actress, who every night abandons her baby in the theater, photographed in real life with a little four-year-old she adores. Except that the four-year-old was such a mass of skin and bones, and so scabby with dirt, they couldn't photograph him. —The next night Mommy had all Paris drenched in tears. The rumor had spread that with her own child at death's door, she'd insisted on going on. The play was a smash. At least I got *something* out of it—she sent me to live in Switzerland like a human being.

COLOMBE. My poor Julien. I never realized.

JULIEN. Thanks to Poet-Mine-Own's throbbing verses. I'm well enough today to serve in the army.

COLOMBE. Is Poet-Mine-Own—?

JULIEN. Yes, Robinet. He calls Mommy "Madame Inspiration" and she calls him "Poet-Mine-Own." You'll get used to it.

COLOMBE. *(After a brief pause)* Do you think she'll do anything for us ?

JULIEN. Not if she can help it. *(Getting up and pacing)* But I don't see how she can—a soldier son and his gallant little wife. She'll have to do something.

COLOMBE. It's not nice to talk that way.

JULIEN. I know. Don't you think I'd like the word "mother" to stand for something—good?

COLOMBE. Why is she so fond of your brother?

JULIEN. To begin with, Edouard's jockey father was the one real love of her life. She still sends him money. *(Sitting on stool)* Edouard learned fast how to get on in the world—he'd hang around the theater getting hugged and kissed, a little angel sucking a lollipop. I remind the old girl of my father—a moody army officer.

COLOMBE. Darling, you aren't always easy to live with, you know. Either you're yelling your head off about something or you refuse to open your mouth. Was your father that way, too?

JULIEN. Apparently he was considered impossible. So honest himself that he made every one else squirm. And like a first-class misanthrope, he carefully fell in love with a woman who could only break his heart. He thought Mother would make him sublimely happy. She did, for three weeks. Then she left him for the juvenile lead.

COLOMBE. And your father killed himself?

JULIEN. *(Getting up)* Yes. Mother was terribly put out.

COLOMBE. Julien, she's still your mother. Don't you think if you tried a little harder—?

JULIEN. No, my love, I don't.

COLOMBE. I'm afraid you're impossible, too.

JULIEN. "Impossible" is an unpatriotic word—don't you dare apply it to a prospective soldier of France.

COLOMBE. If you'd ask your mother, I'm sure with the people she knows you could be deferred.

JULIEN. No thanks. I hate it, but I'll go through with it.

COLOMBE. Just because you hate it?

(He smiles faintly.)

And what about me all that time?

JULIEN. *(Going to her, suddenly gentle)* Darling, you're all I've got. It's going to be hell to leave you— but you wouldn't love me if I walked out on the job just to stay with you.

COLOMBE. Are you crazy? Of course I'd love you.

JULIEN. Well, I can't. You might love me but I'd only hate myself.

COLOMBE. *(With a sigh)* You make everything a problem.

(Voices off stage, up Right. MME. GEORGES rushes in, talking loudly.)

MME. GEORGES. She's here! She downstairs, giving some students her autograph.

JULIEN. Haven't they unhitched her carriage horses and put themseives between the shafts? Aren't they imploring her to let 'em pull her through the streets?

MME. GEORGES. If you're going to start in that way— *(Sympathetically)* Don't, Monsieur Julien. When I see what your brother manages to get with a little flattery—

JULIEN. Georgie, you just feel sorry for *yourself*. I'll handle me.

MME. GEORGES. *(After shaking her head at* COLOMBE*)* Anyway, I'm going to let her know you're here. *(Exits up Right.)*

COLOMBE. *(Going up to* JULIEN*)* Darling, you know what we're here for. Please be nice. Think of the baby—and me.

JULIEN. *(Pricking his ears)* Listen to that—just listen to that. It puffs, it pants, it wheezes, it yanks its damn carcass up step by step—who'd ever believe that on stage it's a young girl, it's youth itself—it doesn't even walk, it floats. That's my mother!

COLOMBE. *(Shouting in protest)* Julien!

JULIEN. Stand at attention! Before you shall appear —the goddess of love of the entire Third Republic— *(Sitting in chair down Right)* I know you go for love; you'll be impressed.

COLOMBE. Darling, I'm frightened.

JULIEN. Oh, it doesn't bite.

COLOMBE. *(Going behind his chair)* It's you I'm frightened of.

*(*MME. ALEXANDRA *appears from up Right of corridor, surrounded by* MME. GEORGES *and a collection of* HAIRDRESSERS, CHIROPODISTS, *etc. Sweeps past* COLOMBE *and* JULIEN *without so much as a look, and bangs into her dresing room.)*

MME. ALEXANDRA. *(Snappish)* My son! Of course not. Tell him I don't care to see him. *(She exits into inner dressing room, Left, followed by her* STAFF. *The inner dressing room door is shut.)*

JULIEN. *(Sits like a stone, aghast, till his mother disappears:Then bursts out)* This is just a little too much! This time I'll show her!

COLOMBE. *(Trying to restrain him)* My darling, calm down. You won't get anywhere by yelling.

JULIEN. Let me go. I feel like yelling. I'd choke if I didn't. Mother! *(He flings himself into her dressing room up Right and goes and knocks at the inner dressing room door, which is locked. Rattles it)* Mother! Let me in! Let me in, or I'll break the door down. *(Rattles on in vain)* Madame Alexandra, if you don't open the door, I'll smash all your imitation china, I'll rip up your fake Persian rugs. Let me in, or it'll cost you a damn sight more than anything I want from you. *(He continues to rattle the door.)*

(In corridor COLOMBE goes and stands behind chair down Right. The inner dressing room door opens a little: the CHIROPODIST appears, clutching it firmly.)

CHIROPODIST. Madame wishes to inform Monsieur that she can't see him. She has a rehearsal.

JULIEN. *(Through the half-open door)* Madame Alexandra, I am calm. I am inconceivably, indescribably calm. But this just happens to be something that I can't go into with your chiropodist.

MME. ALEXANDRA. *(From within)* Tell him to get out of my dressing room and wait in the corridor.

JULIEN. *(Teeth clenched, white with anger; suddenly)* As you wish, Mummy dear. I'll wait in the corridor, Mummy dear. *(He goes out, slamming the door; turns red when he sees COLOMBE trembling)* Was I calm enough for you? *(He sits in chair down Right.)*

(The CHIROPODIST waits there till MME. GEORGES goes out to the corridor; then he locks the door leading to corridor—a sneaky, self-important bit of pantomime—then goes into inner dressing room.)

MME. GEORGES. You sure are making headway, Mr. Julien. I begged you to behave.

JULIEN. Sorry. Frightfully sorry.

MME. GEORGES. After all, it's you that wants the help —you're the one that's got to make the effort.

(The LIGHT in the dressing room comes up.)

JULIEN. Did I walk past *her?* Did I refuse to see *her?*

MME. GEORGES. *(After a second. As she takes stool and starts to return it to room off Right)* How much do you want? Maybe if she knew the amount—

JULIEN. I have to serve my country. I want her to look after my wife and child while I'm away.

MME. GEORGES. *(With a low whistle)* Three years is a long time.

JULIEN. *(Significantly)* Yes.

(During all this, MME. ALEXANDRA has changed into a dressing gown. She comes into dressing room and sits on the armchair Center: the CHIROPODIST takes her foot, the MANICURIST her hand, the HAIRDRESSER her head. GOURETTE, her secretary, stands waiting in doorway Left, papers in hand. There is the sense of an ancient idol companied by Priests.)

MME. ALEXANDRA. *(After a moment)* Gourette!

GOURETTE. *(Advancing obsequiously)* Yes, Madame?

MME. ALEXANDRA. What's the mail?

(In corridor MME. GEORGES puts stool down and goes to dressing room and listens.)

GOURETTE. A bill for your "Goddess of Love" cos-tumes. It's the third one.

MME. ALEXANDRA. Really? What else?

GOURETTE. The stagehands want a raise.

MME. ALEXANDRA. They do? What else?

GOURETTE. The Consumptive Students Aid Society are having a benefit.

MME. ALEXANDRA. I've already given the students.

GOURETTE. These are consumptive students.

MME. ALEXANDRA. Are they students or are they consumptives?

GOURETTE. They say that Madame Sarah Bernhardt sent them a statue she carved herself.

MME. ALEXANDRA. Tell them I'm not a sculptress, like Madame Sarah Bernhardt— I merely act.

GOURETTE. Madame Sarah Bernhardt's gift will get a lot of publicity.

MME. ALEXANDRA. Anything Madame Sarah Bernhardt does gets a lot of publicity. Is it a big statue?

GOURETTE. If it's the one she exhibited at the last Salon, it's about this big. *(Indicates about two feet high.)*

MME. ALEXANDRA. Is that a'l? I'm amazed. *(Calls out)* Georges!

MME. GEORGES. *(In the corridor, to* JULIEN) She wants me. You stay here now—it'll work out all right. *(She goes into the dressing room with her pass-key, closing the door behind her)* Yes, Madame?

MME. ALEXANDRA. What did you do with that great big bronze horror—that thing I never could get rid of?

MME. GEORGES. The naked lady?

MME. ALEXANDRA. The naked lady's a Rodin! Give them a Rodin just because they've got consumption?

MME. GEORGES. Oh—you don't mean the Skeleton?

MME. ALEXANDRA. Tha-a-at's it. Skeleton pulling someone after him.

MME. GEORGES. It's called "Death and the Young Man."—It's at home—in the attic.

MME. ALEXANDRA. *(To* GOURETTE) Send it with my very best wishes.

(MME. GEORGES *sits on pouf Right.)*

GOURETTE. But "Death and the Young Man"—for young men with consumption?

MME. ALEXANDRA. And why not? It's one of the *few* things that'll make them feel how well off they are.

JULIEN. *(Impatient)* If she thinks she can keep me waiting all afternoon—

COLOMBE. Please, Julien, be polite.

JULIEN. *(Goes and knocks at the door.* COLOMBE *goes to him)* Mother!

(The whole dressing room stops dead, waiting for MME. ALEXANDRA'S *next move.)*

MME. ALEXANDRA. *(To* GOURETTE*)* What else?

JULIEN. *(Knocking again)* Mother!

GOURETTE. A young man from Rouen who's seen you three times in "The Goddess of Love" and would kill himself for you.

MME. ALEXANDRA. Good. Thank him. What else?

JULIEN. *(Knocking and shouting)* Mother! Let me in.

(The dressing room stops dead again.)

MME. ALEXANDRA. *(To* GOURETTE*)* What else?

GOURETTE. *(Dead pan)* A line from Mr. Julien, that he's coming home to see you today on very urgent business.

JULIEN. *(Kicking the door)* Mother: I'll keep kicking the door till you let me in.

MME. ALEXANDRA. *(To* GOURETTE, *who has been listening to* JULIEN *with a faint smile)* Did you hear me? I asked, what else?

GOURETTE. *(The smile vanishing)* The firemen, Madame.

MME. ALEXANDRA. What can they want? There's no fire.

GOURETTE. Their annual benefit—

JULIEN. *(Who has gone on kicking the door)*

Mother! Madame Alexandra! If you don't care about me, think of the beautiful paint on the door.

(COLOMBE *tries to stop him; he pushes her away.*)

COLOMBE. *(Dragging him away)* Julien, that's enough—you're being dreadful!

JULIEN. *(Stops; looks at her; quietly)* Oh,—you think I'm awful, too? All right, I'll stop. *(Goes and sits down in chair down Right.)*

(COLOMBE *sits on stool Right.*)

MME. ALEXANDRA. What else?

GOURETTE. What shall I do about the firemen?

MME. ALEXANDRA. Oh—send them all the flowers that came yesterday.

GOURETTE. Flowers, to firemen?

MME. ALEXANDRA. Certainly.

GOURETTE. But they're really rather faded.

MME. ALEXANDRA. They can water them. Watering things is their specialty. *(Gets up)* That's enough for now. I'm tired. I'm going to get ready for rehearsal.

GOURETTE. As you wish, Madame.

(MME. GEORGES *goes to open the door for him with her pass-key, motions to* JULIEN *and* COLOMBE *to wait quietly.* GOURETTE *exits to corridor.* MME. ALEXANDRA *goes into the inner dressing room, followed by her* STAFF. MME. GEORGES *quickly rejoins her. Alone in the corridor with* JULIEN *and* COLOMBE, GOURETTE *changes his tone.*)

(The LIGHT in dressing room goes down to a glow.)

GOURETTE. The bitch!

JULIEN. *(Looking at him)* Yes.

GOURETTE. *(Coming closer, full of hate)* It's been

like that every day for ten years. "Yes, Madame Alexandra." "Quite, Madame Alexandra." "Oh, at once, Madame Alexandra." *(Suddenly, after a cowardly glance at the closed dressing room door)* God damn your stinking soul, Madame Alexandra!—When will I be able to say it to her face?

JULIEN. Any time you care to. You're a free agent.

GOURETTE. You can say that; you're her son. Mama's boy can act up now and then. But Mama's secretary he either says nothing or he says, "Indeed yes, Madame Alexandra"—and with a smile, too. That's part of the contract.—Sometimes, if I don't guess right off exactly what she wants, know how she tells me? Throws a statuette at my face. By now, I've learned to duck—but even then, I have to keep on smiling. What temperament!—she *couldn't* be anything but a genius. We admire her; God, how we admire her. God, how sick we are of admiring her. It's a privilege to serve her—it has to be, it's such a damn lousy living.

JULIEN. Why do you stay?

GOURETTE. Because I need my—two meals a day. They're all I do need, with everything else I have to swallow. "Why do I stay?" Why do you suppose I stay? Why do you come?—If just once I had the guts to—

JULIEN. *(Gets up)* Get out of here. You're disgusting.

GOURETTE. Yes, I know. I'm disgusting, I'm nauseating, I'm a worm, I'm anything you care to call me. But don't worry—someday the worm will turn.—Run along now, kiss Mommy like a good boy. We all have our pride, our principles; we all can be pushed just so far —only, next thing you know, we're bowing right down to the ground. *(He exits up Right with a nasty laugh.)*

JULIEN. *(Remains standing, distraught, then goes to dressing room door—stops. Suddenly)* I'm sick—let's get out of here.

EDOUARD. *(At this moment EDOUARD appears up Right, walking rapidly toward the dressing room.*

Stops, amazed, in front of JULIEN) My God— Julien!
(Spinning him around) Where'd you come from?
(Notices COLOMBE) And who's the young lady?

(COLOMBE *gets up.)*

JULIEN. My wife. My brother Edouard.

EDOUARD. *(Going to* COLOMBE) Oh, of course. I
remember now. Where in God's name have you been—
two years and not even a postcard.

JULIEN. I was in Belleville, giving piano lessons.
And Belleville's not exactly a music center.

EDOUARD. And now you've come to kiss and make
up— *(Smiles)* Want help?

JULIEN. No thanks. We're leaving.

EDOUARD. Come on, let me have a shot at it. I'll make
it easy for you.

JULIEN. Thanks; you're very kind, but we're leaving.

EDOUARD. Need anything? I'm flat myself, from the
horses. But— *(Indicating the dressing room)* —help is
at hand—a mere matter of minutes. *(Going to door)*
Hold on, don't move.

JULIEN. No. We were in the neighborhood, so we
thought we'd call. Madame's not at home. Don't worry,
it doesn't matter. And it was nice to see you. *(Tries to
stop* COLOMBE *from going to* EDOUARD.)

COLOMBE. *(Going to* EDOUARD) Don't listen to Julien,
Monsieur. He's so—proud. He did come to try to see
your mother.

JULIEN. *(Trying to shut her up)* Quit it, Colombe.

COLOMBE. We have a little baby, and Julien's about
to go in the army. We came to ask his mother to look
after us while he's gone.

(JULIEN *moves away to down Right.)*

EDOUARD. *(Incredulous)* You didn't ask to be
deferred?

JULIEN. No. I leave for camp tomorrow.

EDOUARD. And this child stays behind, flat broke and with a baby in her arms? That's what you're here to explain?

COLOMBE. Exactly, Monsieur. And because his mother couldn't see us right away, he insists on leaving.

EDOUARD. I must say, you haven't changed any. *(To COLOMBE)* He's going to make you extremely unhappy, my child.

COLOMBE. I love him, Monsieur.

EDOUARD. I'm sure you do. We all love him. But that needn't stop us from thinking that life isn't quite the torture chamber he makes it.—And if I hadn't come along, he was going to march off straight to camp and save France?—First of all, my hero, we're going to get you deferred.

COLOMBE. *(Going to JULIEN)* Julien, you see!

JULIEN. No, thank you. I don't want to be deferred.

EDOUARD. Of course not! You prefer "left, right, left." Oh it sounds fascinating. And what fun for this charming young lady—she can be all alone in Belleville, washing diapers or trying to find the money for the baby's milk. One can be a patriot, you know, without making one's wife join the breadline. Please, wait five minutes—let me see what I can do. *(Goes into the dressing room, crosses and enters the inner room without knocking, calls out gaily)* Mother darling, I beg you good day!

(JULIEN doesn't move. COLOMBE, with an admiring look at the departing EDOUARD, comes closer to JULIEN.)

COLOMBE. My, he's nice. See, I was right to tell him about us.

JULIEN. Yes. *(Suddenly, in a different voice)* Colombe—listen to me. After tomorrow, you'll be alone here—and life's not quite everything you think it is.

COLOMBE. I know, my darling.

JULIEN. It can be very tough. It has nothing to do with the pretty speeches people make.

COLOMBE. I know. You've told me before.

JULIEN. Now you'll find out for yourself. All the things that impress you about— *(Going above to her Left and with a slight gesture toward dressing room)* —these people, are just for show.

COLOMBE. Yes, Julien.

JULIEN. You can't know what goes with their idea of a good time—or what comes after.

COLOMBE. *(Laughing a little)* I ought to be scared to death?

JULIEN. There's nothing to laugh at.—Yes, you ought to be scared to death.

COLOMBE. Darling, I'll really try to be, if that pleases you. But is "their idea of a good time" really so awful?

JULIEN. Yes.

COLOMBE. Things like someone telling me I'm beautiful and wanting to buy me flowers?

JULIEN. *(Going below to down Right)* Yes.

COLOMBE. But what can be the harm if I say "thank you" for the flowers, and that's the end of it? It doesn't mean a thing—it's you I love.

JULIEN. I know. But it's not going to be simple.

(COLOMBE *turns away.*)

I'll be way off somewhere—if you really love me—

COLOMBE. Darling, I do love you—no one but you.

JULIEN. You don't know how I want to believe you.—Are you listening,—you're not looking at me.

COLOMBE. I'm not looking at you, but I'm listening— very hard.

JULIEN. *(Going to her. His seriousness slightly comic)* If you love me as you say you do, you'll forget about such things.

COLOMBE. *(With a tender little smile: incredulously)* No pretty things or corsages—or even compliments? I can't look around in shops at all the beautiful clothes I can't afford?

JULIEN. *(Unhappily)* No, baby.

COLOMBE. But I don't want you to buy them for me. I just want to look at them. *(Turns to him)* What harm can it do to look at them?

JULIEN. *(Moving away to down Right)* I don't even want you to look at them.

COLOMBE. You're asking something awfully difficult.

JULIEN. Everything good is difficult.

COLOMBE. *(Going to him)* I'd know what you meant if you said I mustn't let any one else buy them for me; but—

JULIEN. *(Sitting in chair down Right, taking her hands)* No, Colombe. Try to see what I mean. You're my wife: when you married me, you were willing to get along with what I could give you; you were willing—weren't you?—to be poor.

COLOMBE. Yes.

JULIEN. I warned you what it would mean—babies keeping us awake at night, your hands all red from washing dishes. You didn't have to agree to it—and yet you did.

COLOMBE. I didn't because I loved you.

JULIEN. I know. But it's not enough to love me. I won't be here. Promise as the two of us did—

COLOMBE. You mean in front of that awful Mayor with his breakfast in his beard? That time doesn't count.

JULIEN. Then promise, as we promised the priest.

COLOMBE. *(Kisses him)* All right, I promise. *(Moving away)* Now are you happy?

JULIEN. *(Gets up)* Cross your heart. *(Spits.)*

COLOMBE. Cross my heart. *(Spits)* But it's not because I promise, you silly— *(Putting her arms around him)* it's because I love you.

JULIEN. No. Don't you see: that's not it. Tomorrow maybe you won't love me. I want it to be because we chose each other, because we've become part of each other.

COLOMBE. *(Half mystified, half hurt)* Then it doesn't even matter that I love you?

JULIEN. Of course it matters, but I mean something more. Look. Please. I could have known somebody else, you could have known somebody else, and loved him for his looks or something. That kind of love we can feel for lots of people, because we're young and need love. You're something different. *(Going above to down Left)* Other people are hard or mean, and the ones that aren't bastards are blockheads. Ever since I was a little kid all they've done is hurt me. I hate them.

COLOMBE. You must admit you don't go out of your way to make friends yourself.

JULIEN. *(Turns to her)* Not that kind of friends. I've built a better world of my own. A world that means you, and that little monkey that just grins at us, before he really lets us knows what he's like.

COLOMBE. He's your son, whatever he's like. *(Going to him)* If he's not everything you want when he grows up, won't you love him anyhow?

JULIEN. *(With a fierce sincerity)* No.

COLOMBE. Then you only love us for our good points: if I lied or stole or something, you wouldn't love me?

JULIEN. I don't know.

COLOMBE. Do you think that means a *thing?* You've got to love me faults and all.

JULIEN. You've only got a few little girl's faults.

COLOMBE. And if someday I had a great many big girl's faults—bad faults—then you wouldn't love me?— And you think that's love?

JULIEN. *(Moving away a step)* Yes.

COLOMBE. Yes—you do. But that's not how I want to be loved. I want to be loved like a woman, not like a little girl. I want you to love everything about me— not just what it's easy to love.

JULIEN. *(Smiling; beaten)* All right, when I get out of the army, I promise I'll love you that way. We'll throw the most god-awful scenes, we'll stage the most terrific reconciliations. But while I'm away, darling, do what I ask: keep away from these people. *(Suddenly, at once comic and touching)* Be the way I like you to be.

COLOMBE. *(Still a little irritated. Turns away)* I always try to—you should know that.

JULIEN. *(Goes above to her Right. Hesitates: then bursts out)* Another thing, Colombe—don't start seeing much of Edouard.

COLOMBE. *(Moving away)* But he's so nice.

JULIEN. *(Savagely)* You mustn't just because he's so nice. If you love me, you won't—because I'm not nice.

COLOMBE. Is that something to brag about? It's nice to be nice.

JULIEN. No.

COLOMBE. *(With a comic little sigh)* Darling, how complicated you make everything! How careful I keep having to be. And it's really so simple— *(Going to him)* —all I want is to be happy. People are nice, if you're nice to them.

EDOUARD. *(Coming back, shouts)* Still there, you love-birds? *(Comes into the corridor, looking pleased)* One for our side, children! She refuses to see the undutiful son but is all agog to meet his wife. Incidentally—what name shall I say?

COLOMBE. *(Like a schoolgirl)* Colombe, Monsieur.

EDOUARD. I *like* it—but what *is* it?

COLOMBE. A saint's name.

EDOUARD. That's too bad. But I'm sure she wasn't a —terribly saintly saint. Took Thursdays off, or something. *(To* JULIEN*)* Sonny, stay put for just five minutes: if Ma sees you now, she'll hit the ceiling. First let's have her warm up to Colombe, then you come on in the second act. You know the scene: the son all humility, the mother all forgiveness. One thing, though —I haven't told her she's a grandma. At her age it could be very dangerous. One of these days we'll have a doctor and nurse in attendance and then break the news.

—How's it all sound?—or is it too much for your Puritan soul?

JULIEN. *(Mumbling)* Thank you, Edouard—you're being very good.

(The LIGHT in the dressing room comes up.)

EDOUARD. No— I'm not good; you know very well I'm not. But I like your wife and you *are* my brother. We have to show a little family feeling once in a while. Come along, Colombe; and stop calling me "Monsieur." Try "Edouard."

(They go into dressing room: COLOMBE *gazes about in admiration.)*

Quite something, isn't it? Ma does know how to give things an air. Of course everything's studiously false. Sit down on this pouf that's doing its damndest to look like Louis XV, and wait for me.

*(*COLOMBE *sits on down Right pouf, tentatively.)*

Buck up. I'll go catch the tiger. *(He goes into the inner dressing room.)*

*(*COLOMBE *and* JULIEN *are each alone, with a wall between them.)*

JULIEN. *(Suddenly goes to the door)* Colombe!

COLOMBE. *(Gets up)* Yes?

JULIEN. You promised!

COLOMBE. *(A little impatiently)* Yes, Julien. Please! *(*COLOMBE *sits down.)*

*(*JULIEN *goes back to his chair.* DESCHAMPS, ALEXAN-DRA'S *co-director in the theatre, and* POET-MINE-OWN *enter up Right in the corridor. They are a matched pair of tophats, frock coats, high collars, moustaches and canes.)*

DESCHAMPS. Perfect!

MINE-OWN. You *really* think so?

DESCHAMPS. It's inspired.

MINE-OWN. *(Fatuously)* I must admit, I think it's quite a good new scene.

DESCHAMPS. Poet-Mine-Own, the last act'll be a sensation. *(Walks in front of* JULIEN*)* Pardon, Monsieur. *(Recognizes him)* Why, it's Julien. What are you doing here?

(They shake hands.)

JULIEN. Waiting for my mother.

(MINE-OWN *moves away to down Left.)*

DESCHAMPS. *(A little uneasy)* She knows you're here?

JULIEN. Edouard's passed on the news.

DESCHAMPS. Please, no fireworks just before rehearsal. We open in a week on the twenty-second— every minute counts. Ask Robinet.
(Notices MINE-OWN's *bristling air.)*
You're not going to greet each other?

MINE-OWN. *(Icily)* I'm waiting.

DESCHAMPS. For what?

MINE-OWN. An apology.

DESCHAMPS. Apology for what?

MINE-OWN. *(Indicating* JULIEN*)* Monsieur knows very well for what.

DESCHAMPS. *(Recollecting)* Oh—the kick in the pants! You mean that's still awaiting settlement?

MINE-OWN. Decidedly.

DESCHAMPS. Julien, say you're sorry. You two can't keep on like this. Ten to one you don't even remember what it was all about.

JULIEN. I remember perfectly.

DESCHAMPS. You sure have changed!—Robinet, *you* show some sense. After all, a kick in the pants isn't like a slap in the face. A kick in the pants is no stain on the honor.

MINE-OWN. *(Primly)* The *seat* of the pants.

DESCHAMPS. *(At a loss)* Oh— Well, maybe the seat of the pants does cast a bit of a stain on the honor.— Julien, you've gotta make the first move.

JULIEN. If I move anything, it'll be my foot. And if it's my foot, I can't guarantee *where* it will move.

(The LIGHT in the corridor starts to go down to a glow.)

DESCHAMPS. *(Shaking his head)* You're absolutely hopeless. Come along, Robinet.
(Enters the dressing room, pulling MINE-OWN— who glares at JULIEN and shows by the way he walks that he fears another kick—after him. Noticing COLOMBE.)
Hello.

MINE-OWN. *(Putting on his monocle: in happy surprise)* Mademoiselle.

DESCHAMPS. You're waiting for Madame Alexandra?

COLOMBE. Yes, Monsieur.

MINE-OWN. *(Flitting about COLOMBE, murmuring to DESCHAMPS loud enough for COLOMBE to hear)* Exquisite, isn't she—absolutely exquisite. *(Aloud)* Haven't we met before, Mademoiselle?

COLOMBE. *(Rather embarrassed)* Yes, Monsieur— two years ago, at the theatre.

MINE-OWN. *(Suddenly remembering; unconsciously puts his hand to his pants seat)* I remember now! Then you're here with— *(Indicates JULIEN, who sat down again, head in hands.)*

COLOMBE. Yes, Monsieur. I'm his wife.

MINE-OWN. *(In a "You'll Need Them" tone of voice)* My very best wishes.

DESCHAMPS. *(Who has been at the inner dressing room door)* You there, Madame Alexandra? Poet-Mine-Own is here with the new scene—it's terrific.

MINE-OWN. *(Simpering with false modesty)* Deschamps goes too far. But I do think you're going to like it.

(MME. ALEXANDRA *bursts in, in a beaded dress, a boa, a parasol, an immense hat.* HAIRDRESSER *stands in the doorway gazing upon her.* MME. GEORGES *comes in, goes above table and sits in up Right of of Center chair.* EDOUARD *follows her and stands Right of small table.* COLOMBE *rises.)*

MME. ALEXANDRA. Where's my wonderful new scene? And the little girl—very nice. Good afternoon, my dear.—Mine-Own!

MINE-OWN. Madame Inspiration!

(They fall into each other's arms.)

MME. ALEXANDRA. My great, great man. When I think what a darling he is, besides being a genius.—I hope you slept well?

MINE-OWN. I couldn't sleep. Your play!

MME. ALEXANDRA. Oh, my play. The Muses have drained my sweet poet. *(Turning to* HAIRDRESSER)

(MINE-OWN *sits in her armchair.)*

A chair, someone—a chair for Poet-Mine-Own.

(The STAFF *scurry about for an armchair for each of them.)*

(She stops them with a gesture) None for me—not today. Just a footstool—to sit at a great man's feet.

MINE-OWN. *(Getting up)* No, no: I won't allow it!

MME. ALEXANDRA. What a darling. Like fresh bread. I must kiss him again.

(They kiss again.)

Wonderful poet!

MINE-OWN. Glorious artist!

MME. ALEXANDRA. *(Suddenly detaching herself: down to earth)* Well then—two chairs.

(They sit down: she in her armchair, MINE-OWN *in chair* HAIRDRESSER *has placed below Left end of table.)*

(She looks at Colombe*)* Why, she's a dream! Of course her hair's all wrong.—I'm listening, Poet-Mine-Own.

Mine-Own. *(Who has pulled a script from his pocket)* This is after the big scene—when Leonore has decided to die.

*(*Colombe *sits down.)*

Mme. Alexandra. I see it all. She lies there, already pale as death. Her dress is draped about her in gigantic folds—

(To Mme. Georges, *who is sewing a costume.)* about twenty-five yards of material.

Mine-Own. I'll begin:

   Moon, dear! Cold planet, lifeless as my heart—

Mme. Alexandra. God, how beautiful! Achingly beautiful!

   —Cold planet, lifeless as my heart!

I know just how to read it. I can give it everything. *(While talking, she never stops. Looking at herself in the mirror. Suddenly, in a different voice)* Lucien, you ass!

Hairdresser. *(Hurrying toward her Right)* Madame Alexandra?

Mme. Alexandra. *(Taking false curls off her head and handing them to him)* Just what are you trying to do to me? I look like a poodle. And what on earth are these curls? Will you please do something about it immediately! Then I want you to go to work on this young lady.—Mine-Own, I'm listening.

Mine-Own.

   Moon, dear! Cold planet, lifeless as my heart
   Wouldst of my woes I make for thee a chart?

Mme. Alexandra. It's very beautiful, Poet-Mine-Own—very classical.

   —make for thee a chart.

Mine-Own.

   Wouldst of my woes I make for thee a chart?

Of the loved one betrayed, the loving one bereft,
Tears for the thief, curses on the theft?

MME. ALEXANDRA.

—curses on the theft.
(Meditates) Quite!

(HAIRDRESSER *places another set of curls on table before her.)*

MINE-OWN.

My love has the midnight, mortuary scent
Of lilies drugged with sleep. Ah, once-content,
Now bitterly unhappy heart, decide—

MME. ALEXANDRA. Magic, sheer magic! You see,
Lucien, you've got to quiet down my curls. *(Rising and going to Cheval glass down Left.)*

(COLOMBE *follows her.* DESCHAMPS *goes above table to Right.* EDOUARD *sits on pouf Right.* HAIRDRESSER *goes and stands above* ALEXANDRA. MINE-OWN *rises and goes to Center.)*

And now young lady, come here, take off your hat.—
Hair very low on the forehead, very high on the neck.
Skin like velvet and she keeps it hidden.—And who
found you that mortifying dress?

COLOMBE. Julien, Madame.

MME. ALEXANDRA. That authority!—Georgie, give
me my jewel box.

(MME. GEORGES *hands it to* HAIRDRESSER.)

Go on, Mine-Own, I'm listening:

Happily unbitter heart, decide!

It's already engraved on my memory. *(To* COLOMBE)
Darling, let me help you, you won't recognize yourself.

MINE-OWN. *(Continuing while* MME. ALEXANDRA *is busy with* COLOMBE)

Now bitterly unhappy heart, decide
To be Life's widow—or be Lethe's bride.

MME. ALEXANDRA. *(Patting him)* Like—alabaster,
dear poet.—Edouard, you have taste— What do you
think of this pretty child now?

EDOUARD. No one would recognize her. Mother, you're a magician.

MME. ALEXANDRA. *(Working on* COLOMBE, *putting necklace and Spanish comb on* COLOMBE*)* Why don't you use jewelry, you little idiot—it's so right for you.

*(*MINE-OWN *gives up and sits in her armchair.)*

COLOMBE. I don't have any.

MME. ALEXANDRA. I didn't either, at your age, but I used to buy things in junk shops—artificial, but better than nothing.

COLOMBE. Julien dislikes artificial jewelry.

MME. ALEXANDRA. Don't mention that name to me. When people get too grand for fake stuff, they should be in a position to buy real.—Mine-Own, it's just shattering! But there's something I want to ask—you know who this child is?

MINE-OWN. *(Rather coldly)* Yes.

MME. ALEXANDRA. It's the wife Julien's saddled me with. He's joining the colors. After all the Bastille Days when I've recited the Marseillaise, you know they'd gladly get him deferred. But Monsieur doesn't wish to be deferred. Monsieur is mad for military life, like his father before him. Of course he leaves his wife in Paris without a sou. She's got to have a job. Mine-Own, as long as you're doing this scene over, you could drop in—four or five lines, somebody who comes to console Leonore—an earth-spirit—or a sister-in-law.

DESCHAMPS. *(Suddenly exploding)* O-o-oh no! A new part the management'll have to pay for! Not today, thank you.

MME. ALEXANDRA. *(A thundercloud)* Will you kindly shut up? Who are you, may I inquire?

DESCHAMPS. I just happen to be co-director here—in charge of money matters, as I recall. Besides you're more than able to look after your own family without me. You get half the take as it is.

MME. ALEXANDRA. *(Striding to him)*
(MINE-OWN *edges out of his seat and goes above armchair.)*
Swine—utter swine! Make him leave— I can't bear having him near me.

DESCHAMPS. We're in production. A cast of thirty-two, and a million costumes. We won't make our expenses as it is: it's out of the question to write in another part just because— *(Almost apoplectic)* —blood is—tighter than water—

MME. ALEXANDRA. All you think of is money. You sicken me. Night after night, I wear myself to the bone, I drag out my guts for your sake.

DESCHAMPS. *(Still raging)* When you do it free of charge I'll be delighted to thank you.

MME. ALEXANDRA. Ho, ho, will you? *(Suddenly wrapping herself in her dignity)* Well— I've a sick headache coming on:—I can't rehearse today. *(Sinks into armchair.)*

DESCHAMPS. *(Alarmed)* Madame Alexandra! We open in a week!

MME. ALEXANDRA. Then we won't open in a week.

DESCHAMPS. But we can't possibly postpone. Your present show won't have a leading man after the twentieth—you know he's going into something else.

MME. ALEXANDRA. We can play it without him.

DESCHAMPS. No, we can't. Even with him, it's a flop. *(Mastering himself)* Madame Alexandra, it's four o'clock. The cast has been waiting downstairs to rehearse since half past two. We've got to open on the twenty-second.

(MME. ALEXANDRA *merely stares.)*
Go down and rehearse— I'll do something about the girl.

MME. ALEXANDRA. *(Inexorably)* Seven francs a performance—matinees, double.

DESCHAMPS. For four lines?

MME. ALEXANDRA. All right, she'll speak twelve

lines. *(Gets up)* You filthy tradesman, I can't think
why we put up with you.

DESCHAMPS. *(Licked)* All right, seven francs—even
if she's invisible.—Only go downstairs now and
rehearse!

MME. ALEXANDRA. *(Turning toward* MINE-OWN)
It's a treasure of a scene.

MINE-OWN. But I'd barely started to read it.

MME. ALEXANDRA. That doesn't matter— I've
guessed the rest. Dear friend, you will throw in a few
lines for this child—she can run through them at the
end of the rehearsal. Georgie, try to find her a dress;
she can't go down there looking like this. *(Sits down
again.)*

DESCHAMPS. *(Groaning)* Please, Madame Alexandra
—they've been waiting since half past two!

MME. ALEXANDRA. *(Inspecting herself in front of
table mirror)* Edouard, you've got a good eye—see that
she looks all right.

EDOUARD. *(Getting up and going into inner room)*
Yes, Mater. *(To* COLOMBE) Come along, young lady.

DESCHAMPS. *(Shouting at* COLOMBE, *who doesn't
move)* Do as you're told: go try that dress on.

(COLOMBE *runs off.* DESCHAMPS *goes out, slamming
     the door; passes* JULIEN *without even seeing him
     in the corridor and goes off down Right.)*

MME. ALEXANDRA. *(In front of her mirror trying on
new curls)* How ducky! Now I don't look a bit like a
poodle.—I look like a seal.

HAIRDRESSER. *(Rushing toward her)* But, Madame
Alexandra—

MME. ALEXANDRA. *(Jumps up)* You deserve to be
killed, but I haven't got time now.—Poet-Mine-Own,
Master Poet! Your scene is torrential. Only, know
what I'd do if I were you?

MINE-OWN. *(Uneasily as he comes to her)* No, dear
friend.

MME. ALEXANDRA. I'd cut out the first six lines.

MINE-OWN. But I only read you eight.

MME. ALEXANDRA. Exactly. I'd start with the seventh; It's so much more—instinctive that way.

MINE-OWN. *(In despair)* But the lilies—

(The LIGHT in the corridor starts coming up.)

MME. ALEXANDRA. *(Exiting the while)* Don't let that worry you. I'll have real lilies standing about in tall vases. That's better you know: always show, when you can, rather than tell.

MINE-OWN. But— My lilies don't come in vases—

(Stunned, he exits after her, the HAIRDRESSER following. They go right past JULIEN, who stands up, white as a sheet. MME. ALEXANDRA either doesn't see him or doesn't want to. ALL exit up Right. MME. GEORGES then comes out and trots over to JULIEN.)

MME. GEORGES. It's all fixed. Madame Alexandra was very nice—made Monsieur Deschamps put her in the show. Monsieur Edouard helped tremendously, too.

JULIEN. *(Raising his head; stammering)* They're p-putting her in the show?

MME. GEORGES. Yes. Monsieur Mine-Own is writing her a part, and she'll get seven francs a performance. You needn't worry now about going away.

JULIEN. *(Gets up suddenly)* And who's going to look after the baby?

MME. GEORGES. Oh, at his age they do nothing but sleep.

JULIEN. *(Fed up)* Georgie, leave me alone.— *(Indicating dressing room)* There's no one there now, I can go in? *(Crosses to dressing soom.)*

MME. GEORGES. Monsieur Edouard's picking her out a dress—they want her to rehearse this afternoon already. *(Shuffling off: mumbling)* She'll get double for matinees. *(Exits up Right.)*

EDOUARD. *(Coming out from inner room, calling back)* Till tonight, Princess? *(Bumps into* JULIEN *in the doorway)* Have a look in. You won't recognize your wife. Georgie tell you it's all set? I gotta run now: will I see you later?

JULIEN. I doubt it.

EDOUARD. The best of luck then, General. And don't worry about Colombe—we'll look after her. *(He goes out.)*

*(*JULIEN *goes into the dressing room and stops.*
COLOMBE *appears in a charming dress, unimaginably altered. She rushes to the cheval glass without even looking at him, and squeals with pleasure.)*

COLOMBE. Julien! Can it be me?

JULIEN. Yes.—At least it's your voice.

COLOMBE. *(In front of the mirror)* You can't imagine what a show they put on! They all talk at once, then they all shriek at once—then they fall into one another's arms.—Julien, they're putting me in the new show. I've got lines, I'm getting a costume. And it's nothing in the dim future— I start right in this afternoon. *(Keeps looking at herself)* It's me—can you believe it, Julien?

JULIEN. *(Who has closed his eyes and doesn't move. In a dull, flat voice)* I don't know what to believe, Colombe.

COLOMBE. *(Stares at herself in the mirror, no longer aware that he is there. Smiles at herself, murmurs in ecstasy)* It's me. It *is* me.

*(*JULIEN *turns around and looks at her as—)*

THE CURTAIN FALLS

ACT ONE

Scene II

SCENE: *A badly lighted empty stage. Some flats, up Left, in disorder. Two foliage wood wings, Left. A prop tree, Right. Three narrow gauze scrim legs hang from a batten—one Left, one Center, one Right. Stage Right, part of the proscenium (running up and down stage) can be seen; there are footlights and draw curtain along with it. The draw curtain at the moment is open, the footlights are unlighted. Down Left a small table with deck of cards; an armchair Right of the table, another chair Left of it. Far back, above the Center gauze leg, and dressed up and leaning on a parasol, stands* MME. ALEXANDRA, *who barks toward the wings Left.*

MME. ALEXANDRA. Well?

SCENE-SHIFTER. *(From above)* No one here yet, Madame Alexandra. They probably thought the rehearsal was for two thirty—the way it usually is.

MME. ALEXANDRA. *(In her noble, grand-mannered enunciation)* Crap! *(Starts roaring and raging up and down the stage, like a caged lion)*
(The stage LIGHTS slowly come up.)
The whoors, the ten-franc whoors. The six-franc markdowns. The four-franc has beens. To keep me waiting—And they want a rrraise!—I'll give them a rrraise! The whoors!—

(A shadow appears timidly between two flats up Left. It is COLOMBE *in her debut dress. She doesn't dare approach* MME. ALEXANDRA, *who is shouting "Whoors" for the last time; turns and sees her. Her*

attitude changes as her voice does—she leans, in
high-romantic style, against her parasol.)
Oh—it's you, dear child. I was—dreaming—

COLOMBE. I'm a little early, Madame Alexandra—
the rehearsal's not till two thirty.

MME. ALEXANDRA. I know. But I like to come
before the rest do, and be alone on the stage with the
great ones who played here once, and are no more. I
dream, I slip out of myself, I murmur an immortal
phrase or two—and then it's rehearsal time. I come
down out of the clouds, and I tuck the past away.

COLOMBE. I'm terribly sorry to have interrupted you,
Madame Alexandra. I'll go back to the dressing room.

MME. ALEXANDRA. Oh, it's just as well— I've dreamt
all I dare for one day. *(Suddenly)* You play cards?

COLOMBE. No, Madame Alexandra.

MME. ALEXANDRA. *(Going to table)* That's too bad,
we could have had a little game while we're waiting
for those lice. I'll tell your fortune instead. *(Sitting
in armchair Right of table)* Here, cut the cards.

(COLOMBE *cuts and sits Left of table.)*

(MME. ALEXANDRA *starts laying them out)* One, two,
three, four, five—a club. That's good. Uhm— Still
better. There's a blond young man and a nice trip
somewhere. Hhm—the blond young man again.

COLOMBE. But Julien's dark.

MME. ALEXANDRA. *Julien?*—you don't suppose
people have their fortunes told to hear about their
husbands? *(Lays out more cards)* You're going to
marry a very important man with scads of money.

COLOMBE. But I'm already married.

MME. ALEXANDRA. That's no way to talk! I've been
married eight times.

COLOMBE. Eight times! *Real* marriages?

MME. ALEXANDRA. Why, I should think so—do I
look half-witted? I *always* married my lovers— I even
married one of them twice. Boulin—the sugar Boulin.
First after his mother died, and then after his father.

COLOMBE To comfort him?

MME. ALEXANDRA. Good God, no! To help him get going with his millions.

COLOMBE. Were you happy with him?

MME. ALEXANDRA. Happy with a husband who refused to bathe?—When he died, I married his son by his first wife—a nice clean-cut boy. He died in my arms and what was left went back to his mother. Unfortunately I couldn't marry her. And she knew nothing about how to handle money and died richer than any of them.

COLOMBE. Are there really people so rich they can buy anything they want?

MME. ALEXANDRA. No, that's the funny part. Poor Boulin—the father— He'd have given millions to say something people would laugh at. Couldn't. He tried—all day long, wherever he went. "How do you do-do-do?" he'd say. Or "Remember me to your children—if they *are* yours." (*Shrugs*) No: with all his money, he couldn't get what he wanted.

COLOMBE. Then what do most rich people do with their money?

MME. ALEXANDRA. They hang on to it.

(*Sees* GOURETTE *come in from down Right.*)
(*Screams at him*) Oh, it's you, you clown!—Is it time for rehearsal?

GOURETTE. (*Down Right of Center*) No, Madame Alexandra: rehearsal's at two thirty.

MME. ALEXANDRA. I'm aware of that.

GOURETTE. The concierge told me you were here, Madame. I was in my office, working on your statement for *Le Matin.*

MME. ALEXANDRA. Oh! Just what am I stating?

GOURETTE. Your opinion of love. The editor just phoned; says that Madame Sarah Bernhardt gave them a most vivid statement.

MME. ALEXANDRA. (*Growling*) I daresay.

GOURETTE. What it came down to was she didn't believe there *was* any such thing.

MME. ALEXANDRA. Then say that I do—that I do with all my heart.

GOURETTE. That's just what I was going to say, Madame Alexandra. May I read it to you:
"This tumult that has always overwhelmed us women, this imperious surge—"

MME. ALEXANDRA. *(Interrupting angrily as she gets up and goes toward him)*

*(*GOURETTE *backs away to Right.)*
You damn fool—do you want to make a laughing-stock of me?
(Cries to MINE-OWN, *who has just come in from Left.)*
My other self! My second voice! *(Going to him) Le Matin* wants to know what I think of love.

MINE-OWN. *(Kissing her hands)* What!—Simply tell them that you *are* love.

MME. ALEXANDRA. I can't tell them that myself. You find me a seemly sentence or two. *(She sits in arm-chair.)*

MINE- OWN. *(Moving to Right of Center)* Certainly. *(Starts)*

Always I have given, and you have given back
Always you shall give, and I will give to you—

MME. ALEXANDRA. *(Interrupting)* Not poetry, my poet, not poetry! They know I don't write poetry.

MINE-OWN. Uhm. Perhaps a pensée—an epigram.

MME. ALEXANDRA. That's it. A nice epigram.

MINE-OWN. Uhm. Well— *(To* GOURETTE*)* Take this down. "For real love to flower, we must first root out of us the black weeds of passion. We must—"

MME. ALEXANDRA. Mine-Own, what are you telling us? Love *is* passion. My *God!*

MINE-OWN. Yes, it—

MME. ALEXANDRA. I was driven mad by love, I drove others mad. Think of Alfonse Sableur flinging himself into the lion cage at the circus. For me! *(In a lyrical actressy tone. Getting up)* How that man loved me! He would die for me—he would kill for me. *(To*

COLOMBE) You're a woman—you'll understand. You love someone else, so to this man you say "No"—you've no choice.—Suddenly there's a terrific roar around you—this—friend has got to his feet, has leapt from the box, has bounded into the cage among the lions. The crowds are in a tumult, but no more than your heart, for all at once you understand. You cry out: "Alfonse, I love you. Come back. I am yours."—Too late!

COLOMBE. They tore him to pieces?

MME. ALEXANDRA. No. He got out. But then I didn't love him any more. He should have taken me right there among the lions—but he let the chance slip through his fingers.

MINE-OWN. How beautiful! How womanly! *(To* GOURETTE) Don't lose a word of it.—And then, dear lady?

MME. ALEXANDRA. We left the circus in silence—my husband and I.

MINE-OWN. And Alfonse?

MME. ALEXANDRA. He rushed off to Monte Carlo and lost four million francs on zero.

COLOMBE. And then put a bullet through his brain?

MME. ALEXANDRA. Not exactly. He married a Rothschild.

MINE-OWN. Miriam?

MME. ALEXANDRA. No, Hannah. The flat one.

COLOMBE. Madame Alexandra. What must one be to be love that way?

MME. ALEXANDRA. Just a woman. I was soul and sex, dreaming and waking. Alfonse—and there were many like him—realized that to hold me the ordinary bourgeois attentions were not enough. He really worked at it, he really made an effort.—One day, when I had no appetite whatever— I used to put my glove on my plate, actually I was trying to reduce— Alfonse, frantic that I wouldn't eat anything, made the waiter at Maxim's bring him a raw rat—and consumed it in front of me.

MINE-OWN. How mad! How male!

COLOMBE. And then you managed to eat a little something?

MME. ALEXANDRA. Eat a little something? After that, I couldn't eat for weeks—ugh!—My dear, it's the perfect way to diet. *(Laughing)* The best part was, Maxim's tacked fifty francs on the bill for the rat.

MINE-OWN. What a woman! *(Going to her. In another tone)* Speaking of rats, I just saw our broker. Do you have any Wagon-Lits stock?

MME. ALEXANDRA. Yes. He advised me to buy it.

MINE-OWN. Well, he just advised me to sell it. It's due to drop. He says to put the money into— It's a secret, *(Going above table)* but if we could go to your dressing room, I could hint—

(She looks at him as she starts to leave the stage with him.)

There's a real killing to be made in *(Lowers his voice)* South American copper.

GOURETTE. *(Just as they are exiting)* Madame Alexandra, how shall I end your statement about love?

MME. ALEXANDRA. What a time to bring up that nonsense again. Don't you see we're discussing serious matters? See me after rehearsal. *(Exits Left with MINE-OWN.)*

GOURETTE. Yes, of course. And after rehearsal— *(Mimics)* "Can't you see how drained I am?" And then tomorrow, when they run Réjane's opinion of love—

MME. GEORGES. *(Who has tiptoed in from up Left carrying a costume)* You might as well go back to your offices. They're on the subject of their investments —we'll be lucky if the rehearsal starts by four.

GOURETTE. *(Muttering)* Why the hell should I worry? *(Exits down Right.)*

MME. GEORGES. We all have money problems, don't we, Madame Julien? The public doesn't know. My neighbors all envy me—"What a life you lead, Madame Georges." You like it?

COLOMBE. *(Lost in reverie)* Oh, yes.

MME. GEORGES. Wouldn't you rather be home with your husband and child darning socks?

COLOMBE. *(Suddenly exclaiming)* No!

MME. GEORGES. *(Looks at her, shrugs, prepares to exit)* Well, I've got to press Madame's goddess robe. Beautiful, but ninety-five pleats.—Oh, here comes our leading man. *(She exits Left.)*

(COLOMBE *gets up.* GAULOIS *makes an imposing entrance from up Right with felt hat, flower in buttonhole, stick.)*

GAULOIS. Good afternoon, my sweet. You the first?

COLOMBE. Madame Alexandra's here, Monsieur Gaulois.

GAULOIS. Our star on time? What next?—I was hoping for a few minutes with you. How're things coming?

COLOMBE. Madame Alexandra says I'm doing all right.

GAULOIS. Your progress is amazing—an awkward moment here and there, but, really, amazing. You must come to my place after rehearsal sometime; we'll go over your part.

COLOMBE. You mean it, Monsieur Gaulois?

GAULOIS. A spot of sherry, a dab of pâté—we'll chat. I've a cute little place— Moroccan. *(Comes closer)* I'm mad about you. I can't sleep any more.

COLOMBE. *(Sitting in armchair)* You ought to sleep.

GAULOIS. I can't. I keep seeing you in front of the fire on my tigerskin rug. I moan all night long like a condemned man. *(Going above table)* I drink and drink to forget, and I only remember. You're always there and I can never quite touch you. *(Sinking in chair Left of table)* Sometimes toward dawn I drop off exhausted—my valet finds me stretched out by the cold hearth.

COLOMBE. *(Dazzled)* You have a valet?

GAULOIS. A Moroccan.

COLOMBE. He must be handsome.

GAULOIS. He has a scimitar at his belt. He stands waiting with folded arms, then serves you without a word.

COLOMBE. He's a mute?

GAULOIS. When he should be, like all good Moroccans—and good valets. So come see for yourself. I'll put on Moroccan dress, too—a great white cloak that I got of an Arab chief. I'll squat in the corner to contemplate you.

COLOMBE. *(Putting her hand on table)* You can contemplate me here, Monsieur Gaulois.

GAULOIS. *(Reaching across for her hand)* No, no. I've been waiting for you all my life.

COLOMBE. Really?

GAULOIS. Always. And you've been waiting for me— I know you have. Has any one else ever loved you like a condemned man?

COLOMBE. No.

GAULOIS. Then you've never *known* love. You've never known yourself.

COLOMBE. But I hardly know you, Monsieur Gaulois.

GAULOIS. You know I love you.

COLOMBE. Julien loves me too.

GAULOIS. No doubt. *(Gets up)* But how? Would Julien roll on the ground for you?

COLOMBE. No. *(Suddenly)* Would you eat a raw rat, just to give me an appetite?

GAULOIS. *(Completely thrown off)* A raw rat? Why a raw rat?

COLOMBE. I just wondered.

DESCHAMPS. *(Enters from up Right)* Ah, Gaulois. Good afternoon.

GAULOIS. Good afternoon.

DESCHAMPS. You know, there's a costume rehearsal this afternoon. Alexandra's already dressed.

GAULOIS. *(Looking glumly at him and seeing through him)* Well, then, Colombe, we'd better get dressed too.

DESCHAMPS. *(Countering)* She has plenty of time;

she doesn't come on till the last act. *(To* COLOMBE)
There's something in your contract I'd like to talk
over with you.

GAULOIS. Oh, of course, the contract!—All right,
see you later. *(Exits up Left.)*

(COLOMBE *moves away to Right of Center.* DESCHAMPS
moves to Left of Center; makes sign GAULOIS *is
gone, then comes back behind Center gauze leg.)*

DESCHAMPS. Come to my office for a minute after
rehearsal. A spot of sherry, a dab of pâté, and we'll
sign our little paper. I know I made a fuss the other
day—but that was just for effect. Don't worry, you
shall have your seven francs. Would you like some of
it in advance?

COLOMBE. *(Coming to him)* Oh—could I?

DESCHAMPS. Come in after rehearsal—and you
needn't say anything to Madame Alexandra; she
counts her pennies, you know. I'm an easy mark.

COLOMBE. Thank you, Monsieur Deschamps—
You're very kind.

DESCHAMPS. *(Moving toward her.)*
    (She backs away.)
Not with everybody. Not with everybody. Tell me—is
that your only new dress?

COLOMBE. Yes.

DESCHAMPS. We can't have that! I know just the
dressmaker who could make you just the thing—a little
suit, maybe in that walnut color they're showing.

COLOMBE. Uhm—but wouldn't you think a little fur
cape with a hat to match? I saw one on the Rue de
Rivoli this morning.

DESCHAMPS. *(Taken aback)* Oh—! Well, perhaps
trimmed with fur.

COLOMBE. *(Moving away below tree)* Only what can
I buy on seven francs a day?

DESCHAMPS. *(Follows; softly)* We'll work it out,
between the two of us.

COLOMBE. You're terribly kind, Monsieur Deschamps.

DESCHAMPS. I really am, you know, in spite of my reputation.

MINE-OWN. *(Entering)* Where's my little, where's my little, where's my little nymph?

DESCHAMPS. *(Frigidly)* Right here. With me.

MINE-OWN. *(Stops down Left of Center)* You know, Deschamps, I can't get her out of my mind. Last night I wrote eight more lines for her.

COLOMBE. For me?

MINE-OWN. All for you. I couldn't sleep a wink thinking of you.

COLOMBE. You, too? Nobody around here is able to sleep.

MINE-OWN. What do you mean?

DESCHAMPS. Robinet, you know how long the play is. You can't make it longer.

MINE-OWN. My dear Deschamps, this child is going to be a sensation.

DESCHAMPS. Of course; she's wonderful. But she doesn't come on till the very last scene when the women are putting on their gloves.

MINE-OWN. *(Going above tree to* COLOMBE'S *Right)* For once, leave it to me. I'll work with her on her part. After the rehearsal, Colombe, you come to my apartment for a spot of sherry, and then we'll go to work.

DESCHAMPS. She's tied up after the rehearsal.

MINE-OWN. *(Going to him)* That's too bad; this comes first. We open next week—this child has to work, Deschamps.

DESCHAMPS. She's also got to sign her contract.

MINE-OWN. That takes days, doesn't it? Go get it, and she'll sign it now.

DESCHAMPS. It's being drawn up now.

MINE-OWN. The play opens in a week, and this child's part can make or break it.

EDOUARD. *(Who has come in from down Left and*

overheard; smiling) I've the solution for all of you. Since Colombe can't perform stark naked—mu h as we regret the fact—and there's just time enough, after rehearsal, to order her a dress, I'll take over. Her date will be with the dressmaker— *(Smiling at them* BOTH) That is, if you *really* want to open on the twenty second.

DESCHAMPS. All right, maybe that's the best idea. See you all later. *(Exits up Right.)*

MINE-OWN. *(Pacing up and down)* The theatre is a great institution, when everything else comes ahead of the script.

EDOUARD. *(Still smiling)* Mine-Own, Mother's looking for you.

MINE-OWN. *(Unwilling to leave)* I just this minute left her.

EDOUARD. Since then, she's been deep in thought— and decided the new scene is too long.

MINE-OWN. Too long? Why, all she's done is cut it.

EDOUARD. After deep thought, she only likes the very last line.

MINE-OWN. Only one line! And what, pray, is only one line to rhyme with?

EDOUARD. I can't tell you yet— I haven't had time to work it out.

MINE-OWN. This is too much. Who wrote this play?

EDOUARD. Dozens of people say you did.

MINE-OWN. *(Like a madman)* I'll take it off the boards. She—she can have the last line, but we'll see who has the last word! *(Exits up Left.)*

COLOMBE. This is ghastly. What'll they do?

EDOUARD. Nothing whatever. This is the theatre— while they're rehearsing a drama, they're also playing a farce. *(Changing his tone)* The important thing is that I rescued you from those two old goats. *(Looks at her)* Or do you find them fun?

COLOMBE. *(As she goes and sits on base of tree)* I do in a way. They sniff, and circle round me, and roll their eyes, and say they can't sleep at night.

EDOUARD. Who can't sleep at night?

COLOMBE. Monsieur Gaulois and Monsieur Poet-Mine-Own.

EDOUARD. Deschamps can?

COLOMBE. Yes, Deschamps can. But he wants to give me an advance on my salary. And a little walnut-colored suit.

EDOUARD. And what decision have you reached?

COLOMBE. The suit might be very attractive.

EDOUARD. *(Going to her)* Come, come, my sweet. Don't look so innocent. I mean, which benefactor?

COLOMBE. There's only one. The others only offer their insomnia and a little sherry.

EDOUARD. It's just as well I'm here to stand guard over honor.

COLOMBE. What honor?

EDOUARD. The family's. I'd hate to have to slap all three faces—I don't mind getting killed so much, but to have to get up three times at five a.m.!

COLOMBE. *(Getting up and moving to down Right)* You're the one with the evil thoughts: they only want to help me with my part.

EDOUARD. They do? That's the best they could think up?

COLOMBE. *(Turns to him)* Didn't you think up the same thing? Didn't I go to your place?

EDOUARD. *(Going to her)* Yes, but for the sake of your career. To prove it, I didn't even offer you sherry.

COLOMBE. I noticed.

EDOUARD. Just the script—read standing up in the dining-room. It's not that I'm a moralist—but sipping sherry side by side on a divan: I don't think I could manage that.

COLOMBE. I'm afraid that's too deep for me.

EDOUARD. Really? Well, then, my sweet: when I have fun, I have fun; and when I guard the family honor, I guard the family honor.

COLOMBE. Since we're going to order my dress this evening and I can't come to your place, couldn't we rehearse my part now instead of talking foolishness?

EDOUARD. Of course. *(Reaching in his pocket and going to table)* Here's my script: I'm never parted from it.

(The LIGHTS begin to dim down, stage Right.)

COLOMBE. I'm sure this bores you to death.

EDOUARD. Frightfully.

COLOMBE. I can always ask Monsieur Gaulois—it might not bore him.

EDOUARD. No, perhaps it wouldn't. So *I'd* better suffer. *(As he places armchair to face her)* Let's do the end first: it wasn't right yesterday. *(He sits—she crosses toward him.)*

COLOMBE. "And if I were to tell you I loved you?"

EDOUARD. "I wouldn't believe it."

COLOMBE. "And if I were to tell you I'm sick at heart?"

EDOUARD. *(Putting script on table)* "With eyes like yours?"

COLOMBE. "What do you know of my eyes—when you never look at them?"

EDOUARD. *(Getting up and taking her in his arms)* "Never?"

COLOMBE. *(Lets him look at her, then turns bashfully away)* "Not so hard, Monsieur—you make me blush."

EDOUARD. "You thought to play at love, and now are caught in its snare. You yearn, as much as I, for the kiss I'm about to take."

COLOMBE. *(Letting her head fall on his shoulder)* "Yes, Baron."

EDOUARD. *(Looking at her for a moment over his shoulder, backing away, then sighing in another tone)* The Baron—kisses you.

COLOMBE. *(Without moving)* Was it any better than yesterday?

EDOUARD. Yes, my angel. You little devil, where did you learn all this?

COLOMBE. I just speak the way I feel.

EDOUARD. Do you do it so well by imagining you're with Julien?

COLOMBE. *(Moving away a little)* Julien would never talk to me like that.

EDOUARD. Gaulois?

COLOMBE. No.

EDOUARD. But you still think that you're yourself—Colombe?

COLOMBE. *(Moving away to down Right of Center)* Yes.—A Colombe who loves the Baron.

EDOUARD. And when we do the farewell scene, you'll feel terribly unhappy?

COLOMBE. Not really. Though I'll really want to cry.

EDOUARD. *(Going to her)* Has Julien ever made you cry?

COLOMBE. *(Looks at him)* Yes, sometimes.

EDOUARD. And when you cry, while you're acting, it's those tears you think of?

COLOMBE. *(Looks away)* No. It's not the same.

EDOUARD. But you really cry?

COLOMBE. I cry, but I'm not really sad—deep down.

EDOUARD. But when you cry with Julien—you're really sad, deep down?

COLOMBE. Yes—that's real life.

EDOUARD. You're sure you've never cried with him *without* being really sad, deep down?

COLOMBE. *(Looks at him)* Why do you ask that?

EDOUARD. For my own good. I just can't believe that anyone who cries so heartbreakingly whenever she feels like it, wouldn't sometimes decide that she feels like it.

COLOMBE. *(Turns to him)* You mean I'm a liar?

EDOUARD. What a horrible word!—But women do have their own patented way of telling the truth: *(Going back to armchair)* only backwoods idealists like Julien wouldn't know that.

COLOMBE. *(Going up to him)* I don't like you to speak that way of Julien.

EDOUARD. Why?

COLOMBE. He's a real man.

EDOUARD. I know—and women love real men. They need them for the kind of game they play. With bad eggs like me, they know that kind of thing won't work. But it can still be fun.

COLOMBE. Fun?

EDOUARD. With people like me. You can drop the mask and relax. It must be terribly wearing to always have to be a womanly woman.

COLOMBE. *(Breaks out laughing and moves away a little)* Edouard, you really *are* a bad fellow.

EDOUARD. *(Moving away and sitting in armchair)* Of course!—Well, shall we do the scene once more before the high priests of art take over the stage?

COLOMBE. *(Places herself)* Suppose Monsieur Gaulois discovers me in your arms?

EDOUARD. I'm sure he'll know we're only rehearsing a scene.

COLOMBE. "And if I were to tell you I love you?"

EDOUARD. "I wouldn't believe it."

COLOMBE. "And if I were to tell you I'm sick at heart?"

EDOUARD. "With eyes like yours?"

COLOMBE. "What do you know of my eyes—when you never look at them?"

EDOUARD. "Never?" *(Gets up, takes her in his arms and is about to kiss her—suddenly murmurs)* You little devil! *(Lets her go; says with a childlike softness that cuts under his man-of-the-world air)* Even so, we mustn't hurt Julien!

(They stand against each other without daring to look each other's way.)

CURTAIN

ACT TWO

SCENE I

SCENE: *The dressing room and corridor, as in Act I,
Scene I, but looked at from the reverse side. The
door of Mme. Alexandra's dressing room is up
Left. Down Left is the door of Gaulois' dressing
room. Colombe's room is Right, the door to it is
Center in Left wall. The whole Left side and front
of Colombe's dressing room is exposed. The corridor runs from up Center to down Left and off. Up
Center are two steps leading to the stage. Two
steps down Right lead to the corridor that is off,
down Left. A small railing from far Left to the
steps on the platform. A chair Left on the platform. In Colombe's room, there are a small dressing table and mirror, Right against the wall. A
small pouf, Left of table. Down Right a built-in
closet. Up Center, an alcove; between the alcove, a
small screen; and below the screen, a small bench.
Down Left a basket of flowers. MME. GEORGES is
in the chair Left. JULIEN, in uniform, paces back
and forth; opens Colombe's dressing-room door.*

JULIEN. Is this hers?

MME. GEORGES. Yes.

JULIEN. *(Closing the door)* There was no one at the
house.

MME. GEORGES. To come back like this without a
word! We didn't expect you, Monsieur Julien.

JULIEN. *(Pacing up and down)* We suddenly got a
twenty-four-hour pass because there's a new General.

MME. GEORGES. Is the new one nicer?

JULIEN. They're all alike.

MME. GEORGES. Now don't act the way you usually do. Tip your hat when you pass him.

JULIEN. And be led out and shot?—She didn't even go home for dinner!

MME. GEORGES. You know the theatre—her time's not her own.

JULIEN. There was a woman at the house—someone she pays to watch the baby.

MME. GEORGES. She's a very good mother—spends her last sou on the baby. You know she got a raise?

JULIEN. A raise? *(Quickly)* Oh yes, I know!

MME. GEORGES. Ten francs a day now. And a bigger part. I s'pose she's written you all the news here—

JULIEN. She wrote that—

MME. GEORGES. *(Breaking in)* "Eve and the Serpent" was a flop. Monsieur Poet-Mine-Own and Madame Alexandra swore and cursed at each other— I don't know where people in their circle learn such language. Well, then they made up and now they have have a hit— "The Realm of Passion"—the dresses take ten minutes to hook up.

JULIEN. And she comes on late?

MME. GEORGES No, she's on at the start—she'll be here any minute. Unless Monsieur Edouard took her to dinner and brings her back in a cab.

JULIEN. Edouard takes her to dinner?

MME. GEORGES. Sometimes. So does Monsieur Gaulois. That's very unusual for a leading man. But he couldn't be nicer.

JULIEN. *(Coming down the steps to down Left)* I see.

MME. GEORGES. A little thing like that who's all alone, everyone feels sorry for her.

JULIEN. I can believe it.

GOURETTE. *(Enters from* ALEXANDRA'S *room. Shouting)* Curtain in ten minutes! Curtain in ten minutes!

MME. GEORGES. No! Madame's not here—and neither is Mrs. Julien.

GOURETTE. *(Coming down)* That's not my lookout—I've enough to worry about. *(Shouts)* Curtain in ten minutes!

(MME. GEORGES *goes into* ALEXANDRA'S *room.*) *(Sees* JULIEN; *changes his tone)* Ah, Mr. Julien! This is a surprise—you managed to get off?

JULIEN. As you see.

GOURETTE. Army life's getting to be quite a snap. Not like in my day.

JULIEN. Yes. *(After a second)* I got your letter.

GOURETTE. *(Half blushing, half sneering)* So soon?

JULIEN. Last night. Thanks for writing.

GOURETTE. I thought you'd want to be up on the latest stage gossip.

JULIEN. Yes.—Got five minutes to go out for a drink?

GOURETTE. No; it's too close to curtain time. And I have to dress— I have to fill in, somebody got sick.

JULIEN. *(Seizing him by the arm)* Then let's go in here— I'll only be a minute.

(The LIGHT in the dressing room comes up.)

GOURETTE. I know. But I ought to warn you, it's her dressing room.

(They go into COLOMBE'S *dressing room. A voice calls "GEORGIE!")*

MME. GEORGES. *(Coming into corridor)* Yes, Monsieur Gaulois?

GAULOIS. *(Appears at the entrance to his dressing room in a Moroccan robe and his shorts, putting on make-up)* Would you fix my shirt?—Has our little one come?

MME. GEORGES. Not yet. But I've a surprise— Monsieur Julien is home on leave.

GAULOIS. No!

MME. GEORGES. *(Going into his room with him)* I

told him how nice you've been about his missus. *(She closes the door.)*

JULIEN. *(In* COLOMBE'S *dressing room,* JULIEN *has been listening to them: Now he grabs* GOURETTE *by the collar)* Who is it?

GOURETTE. That's *it!* It'd be fine if we knew right off—but that's the tough part about having an unfaithful wife: who's she unfaithful with?

JULIEN. Tell me or I'll beat your brains out.

GOURETTE. You're all alike— "I'll strangle you." "I'll murder you." The sure sign of the beginner! It's not that simple, you know. It's a real part, it's one of the established roles—the romantic lover, the heavy father, the deceived husband. You've got to learn the lines, you've got to know the cues. It's an art, a very great art, and it takes time.

JULIEN. *(Taking him by the throat)* God damn you, cut that out—tell me, or I'll kill you.

GOURETTE. That'd be fine training: you wouldn't even get to be an understudy— I know: you want to prove your virility— It's useless. Stop choking me, Monsieur Julien—it's not me, you can be sure of that.

JULIEN. *(Letting him go, taking hold of himself)* Why did you write to me?

GOURETTE. Because I like you—and because this made us—colleagues.

JULIEN. You don't know who it is?

GOURETTE. No.

JULIEN. *(A second, then* JULIEN *sits on bench)* Who's she been going out with?

GOURETTE. Ah, now we're getting somewhere. That's sound: a good cuckold should be methodical. I can only help in small ways, you know— The brilliant hunches, the inspired detective work will have to come from you.—There are four candidates.

JULIEN. *(With a start)* Four?

GOURETTE. Four possibilities, that is; I didn't mean four certainties. Edouard, Gaulois, Poet-Mine-Own, and our master of the revels, Monsieur Deschamps. A lovable group, aren't they? I think you can skip the hairdresser—though he does do her hair an awful lot, and women go for him.

JULIEN. The man has a smell.

GOURETTE. The animal in him—which you shouldn't minimize; that could be part of his appeal. One of the first rules of your new profession is: don't go by what *you* feel, by any ideas *you* have in the matter. That's exactly why most cuckolds—flunk.

JULIEN. Five with the hairdresser!

GOURETTE. Don't be upset. I know a Captain who suspected his entire company. Think what a Colonel would have to go through.

JULIEN. I'll strangle all five of them!

GOURETTE. Yes, you can—but it won't do any good. You won't get relief even if the guilty one's among them.

JULIEN. She'll be back any minute— I'll worm it out of her.

GOURETTE. You good little boys, how you all go about it. You'll never learn *anything* that way.

JULIEN. *(Groaning)* But Colombe loves me.

GOURETTE. She may. But it won't help.

JULIEN. I left her, like an imbecile, with this stinking gang. She's just a baby.

GOURETTE. Uhm. The trouble with babies, we can't read their minds.

JULIEN. What should I do?

GOURETTE. *(Sitting beside him)* Now you're starting to show promise. Begin by studying the classics in the field: it's going to be very strange at first.—In a minute she'll come in, she'll smile, she'll kiss you: watch out, it'll all seems terribly normal. But life gets very odd for the cuckold: strange coincidences start piling up as they never used to. The letters that don't come, or come too late. The phones that ring—and there's no one at the other end. The friends you haven't seen in years who stick like a leech for a whole afternoon: all the things in ordinary life that you can't quite dope

out—they're suddenly crystal clear! Nothing will be
mysterious. The alibis will be perfect—terrifyingly
perfect. There was something hearteningly ambiguous
about the old life: now there's an answer for everything. Only every answer will breed ten new questions.
The gas man who rings the bell won't just be the gas
man—he'll be a question. The song she's humming, the
article she's reading—questions. The new color of her
lipstick—a tremendous question. Life will be a long
weaving snake dance of questions; and you yourself
will become an eavesdropping, dresser-drawer rummag-
ing, sounds-in-her-sleep-pondering—question mark.

JULIEN. No! I'll ask her nothing.

GOURETTE. *(Getting up)* Oh, yes, you will! And
when you're all finished, you'll have barely started.
Now you'll begin on yourself—questioning yourself,
doubting this, doubting that, finally deciding you
invented it all. That day you will be the real thing—
     (VOICE off stage up Center.)
a *cordon bleu* among cuckolds. *(Listens)* Here she
comes! Make up your mind, Monsieur Julien: either
you want help and listen to me; or you can be your own
lawyer and see what happens.

JULIEN. What shall I do?

GOURETTE. To begin with, hide. That's another rule:
always hide.

JULIEN. *(Looking frantically around—the VOICES
outside come nearer)* Where?

GOURETTE. *(Opening the closet and pushing him
inside)* In the closet—headquarters for cuckolds!
     *(He has pushed him into the closet, now rushes
     out into the corridor; cries.)*
On stage for Act One! On stage for Act One!

MME. ALEXANDRA. *(Rushing in up Center, followed
by her STAFF)* Stop bellowing like that, you half-wit!
The curtain'll go up when I'm ready.—Are you doing
Doussin's part again tonight?

GOURETTE. Yes, Madame Alexandra.

MME. ALEXANDRA. *(Disappearing into her dressing*

room, followed by STAFF) That'll be a treat for the audience.

(GOURETTE *goes down to steps and off down Left.*)

COLOMBE. *(Entering up Center with a cry)* Where is he? Where is he? *(Goes to her dressing room, sees no one, runs out)* Georgie, Georgie! Where's Julien?
    (Goes back, sees JULIEN, *who has come out of the cupboard.)*
My darling! Where did you come from?
    JULIEN. The closet.
    COLOMBE. What were you doing in there?
    JULIEN. Playing a little joke on you.
    COLOMBE. *(Throws herself into his arms. Squeezing him tight)* This is wonderful— It's been *so* long!
    JULIEN. *(Gently)* Longer than you can imagine.
    COLOMBE. But you've been busy. All the things you had to learn, while your little wife's been all alone, waiting for you.—This is so nice. And how handsome you look in uniform: like a General.
    JULIEN. Not yet—though there are rumors.
    COLOMBE. *(Seating him on pouf)* Sit down, I'll bet you're tired. *(She sits on his knees)* What's the most you have to march at one time?
    JULIEN. Twenty-five kilometers.
    COLOMBE. But they let you take a street-car home?
    JULIEN. No.
    COLOMBE. And all the other things you have to do. I'll bet you don't have time to think of me.
    JULIEN. Plenty of time.
    COLOMBE. Of course you'd say so. But when you're not working and you're sitting around with the boys— it's a vacation, too. Good riddance to wives. If the girl back home is cold she should take a hot water bottle to bed.
    JULIEN. How's the baby?
    COLOMBE. Oh, he's fine.—Do you like my little walnut-colored suit?

JULIEN. Uhm hmm—very nice. And I bet expensive.

COLOMBE. No, not a bit. I found a dressmaker who gives you a price and lets you pay so much a week. Anyhow, I'm quite a moneymaker now. I'll be able to treat you so you can have fun and treat the girls. We know all about you—think we didn't know why you refused to be deferred?

JULIEN. There are very few girls around camp, Colombe.

COLOMBE. There are enough. I'm sure you were unfaithful.

JULIEN. But I wasn't. *(In a natural tone)* And you?

COLOMBE. Me? Darling, don't be silly: I wouldn't have even had time. I've got a pretty big part in the new play: I've had to work my head off. Are you going to come and applaud me? Knowing you're out front'll give me stage fright, but still — Oh, baby, my big sweet baby, it's wonderful to have you back. And you look so well!

JULIEN. Do I?

COLOMBE. *(Kisses him, stands up)* Being without you does have its good side: it makes it so wonderful to be together again.—Will you forgive me if I dress? —We ring up any minute. I'm late. *(She goes in alcove up Center behind the screen. While she undresses, you see her naked arm throw one bit of clothing after another onto screen. Calling out)* How long is your leave?

JULIEN. Twenty-four hours.

COLOMBE. Is that all? Couldn't you say you missed your train?

JULIEN. No.

COLOMBE. But darling, that's awful. I've been invited out after the show by some people who can do a tremendous lot for me—it would take too long to explain—and tomorrow I have to rehearse all afternoon.

JULIEN. It's very simple—you break your date.

COLOMBE. Oh, Julien, baby, I just can't—my whole future's involved.

JULIEN. So is mine. And a military future can be mighty brief.

COLOMBE. Don't talk that way.—You'll have other leaves, but I may never have another chance like this. These are very big people who could get me into the Folies-Bergère. They need somebody my type for a sketch in the next revue. Don't worry, darling, I'll wear clothing—otherwise I wouldn't even consider it.

JULIEN. *(Getting up, shouting suddenly)* Stop talking such slime. Colombe, you're coming home with me tonight.

COLOMBE. *(After a silence)* It's sure like old times. You've just come back and you're screaming already!

JULIEN. Yes, I'm screaming—and I'll scream worse if I have to. But I know this much : you're not going in for the kind of thing you're talking about.

COLOMBE. *(Appears in panties and corset from behind the screen. Innocently; hands across her breasts)* What are *you* talking about?

JULIEN. Stop playing dumb.

COLOMBE. But I'm not, baby; really I'm not.

GAULOIS. *(Comes out of his dressing room, two-thirds dressed, and knocks at* COLOMBE'S *door)* Are you there, my little monkey? I wanted to tell you to watch your step. *(He half opens the door, sees* JULIEN*)*
     *(*COLOMBE *runs behind screen.)*
Oh, forgive me.

JULIEN. Forgive *me*.

GAULOIS. Enjoying your leave?

JULIEN. Immensely.

GAULOIS. Good!—You know the new scene?

COLOMBE. Yes, Monsieur Gaulois.

GAULOIS. Good! We're using it tonight. *(Goes back to his dressing room.)*

(COLOMBE *comes out.)*

JULIEN. Why does he call you his little monkey?

COLOMBE. I don't know. He's got a nickname for everybody— He's helped me a lot with my part.

DESCHAMPS. *(Now* DESCHAMPS *rushes in up Center, self-importantly; taps discreetly on* COLOMBE'S *door)* Are you there, my little titmouse?

JULIEN. Now it's a titmouse.

DESCHAMPS. I just wanted to tell you to watch your step. *(Has opened the door—sees* JULIEN.)

(COLOMBE *runs behind screen.)*

Oh—sorry.

JULIEN. *So* sorry.

DESCHAMPS. Awfully sorry. I wanted to tell your wife something.—Everything all right?

JULIEN. Everything's all right.

DESCHAMPS. You look fine.

JULIEN. Thanks. That's what everyone says.

DESCHAMPS. *(To* COLOMBE) I just wanted to tell your wife— We're going up on time tonight! Don't be late. *(He trots off up Center.)*

JULIEN. Little titmouse. From that idiot. God, he's awful.

COLOMBE. *(Coming out again)* There you go. You have to see the worst in everything. They shouldn't think of me as a little monkey, they shouldn't think of me as a little titmouse: what *do* you want them to call me— "Madame la Duchesse"?

JULIEN. How could you make friends with such idiots?

COLOMBE. I haven't made friends with them. I see them every day— I have to work with them. Nobody else is so disagreeable about nothing the way you are. Anyhow, they amuse me.

JULIEN. Don't say that: they can't.

COLOMBE. Why can't they?

JULIEN. Because I know you too well.

COLOMBE. *(With a cool look as she sits on pouf)* Are you sure?

*(MME. GEORGES comes out into corridor and goes to
COLOMBE's door.)*

JULIEN. Yes. And in the end you'll go back to being
yourself, whether you want to or not.

COLOMBE. *(Facing him with the look of an enemy)*
My poor Julien.

MME. GEORGES. *(Tiptoeing in)* Glad to see one
another?

JULIEN. Tickled to death.

MME. GEORGES. It's nice to come back to a wife that
everybody raves about, but who's just for you.

(COLOMBE gets up and goes to her.)
(She tightens laces on her corset) Look at that little
figure, Monsieur Julien—you could eat her up. And
what a hit she's made. Aren't you happy to have such
a big success of a wife?

JULIEN. I could puke from joy.

MINE-OWN. *(Appears from up Center in the corridor, knocks discreetly on COLOMBE's door)* Are you
there, my little turtle-dove?

JULIEN. *(Goes to door and shouts)* Yes, I'm here!

MINE-OWN. *(Jumping at man's voice)* Forgive me
—do please forgive me.—I just wanted to tell you to
watch your step. *(Stops)* Forget it, it's nothing— I
don't know what I'm saying, I'm so nervous—the King
of Spain's out front. Act your best tonight, dear little
lady—and do forgive me. *(Trots away out up Center.)*

JULIEN. Now it's a turtle-dove. What is this: Aesop's
fables? How could you let that slimy old character call
you his turtle-dove: I told you never to speak to him.

COLOMBE. But he wrote the play I'm in.

JULIEN. Isn't it enough to have to speak his lines?—
And why do they all want you to watch your step?
Count of me—hmm?

COLOMBE. For heaven's sake can't you ever let up?

JULIEN. And you smile at them, and purr at them—
(Springing toward her) Wipe off your mouth: I can't
stand the way you look.

(COLOMBE *cries out and falls on pouf.*)

MME. GEORGES. *(Stopping him)* Mr. Julien, you'll ruin her make-up. It's her job right now to smile. Look at her—crying. Imagine what'll happen if it drips on her mascara!

JULIEN. Georgie, get out.

MME. GEORGES. Not if you're going to make her cry!

JULIEN. *(Taking her arm and throwing her out)* Damn you, when I say get out—you get out.

(JULIEN *comes back.* MME. GEORGES *puts her ear to the door and gradually, during the scene, the* HAIRDRESSER, CHIROPODIST, GAULOIS, MANICURIST, GOURETTE *in Louis XV costume, and most of the cast, a* BOY *and* GIRL *dancer, silently collect in the corridor behind* COLOMBE'S *door.*)

JULIEN. *(Suddenly)* Who is he?

COLOMBE. Who is what?

JULIEN. Your lover.

COLOMBE. Please, Julien, stop it. I haven't got a lover.

JULIEN. *(Grabs her: wildly)* You tell me who it is!

COLOMBE. Darling, how can I tell you something I don't know?

JULIEN. It's no use, Colombe: I've got proof. Somebody saw you—and wrote and told me.

COLOMBE. *(Freeing herself: furious)* Who dared to write you?

JULIEN. See—you're scared. There's no use acting innocent. I've a letter on me giving the whole story. *(Mimics the* OTHERS) —My little snake.

COLOMBE. I want to know who wrote you.

JULIEN. I'm sure you do.

COLOMBE. An anonymous letter no doubt. They all hate you in this business, they're all jealous. Go on, act like a detective, now that you've started all this: ask the janitor, ask the old man who walks the dogs, ask the old woman who mops up the men's room—you'll hear plenty of stories. I won't have one lover, I'll have twenty. They're only happy spreading filth. Anonymous letters while they sit around waiting for parts they'll never get. You'd think you'd know better after being raised in this atmosphere. But you'd rather believe *them* than show a little confidence in your own wife. They don't even have to sign their names. *(Changes her tone: close to tears)* Those two glorious years when we were broke and I cooked and cleaned and did everything I could to make you happy—*then* you never questioned my fidelity. Do you think this is the first time men have paid attention to me? Do you think if I'd wanted to be unfaithful I had to wait for you to go in the army?—It never once entered my head, even when we went without dinner and pretended we'd just come back stuffed from Maxim's. Go on, forget all that, just roll me around in the mud. *(She falls sobbing on pouf.)*

JULIEN. *(Doesn't move)* I'm sorry.

COLOMBE. You're sorry—you're sorry! It's done now. You'd believe any one rather than me.

JULIEN. *(Sitting on bench)* I want to believe you.

COLOMBE. *(In a low, colorless voice. From beneath her tears)* The letter was signed?

JULIEN. Yes.

COLOMBE. Tell me her name.

JULIEN. It was a man.

COLOMBE. *(Thinks for a minute: exclaims)* Oh, now I see! It would never occur to you that this—pig wrote the letter out of spite, because I wouldn't agree to his charming proposals?

JULIEN. *(Leaping up)* Who wanted you to?—Tell me his name!

COLOMBE. No—you tell me, so I can see whether he's the one. Let me just guess the first letter. It's a P, isn't it?

JULIEN. No.

COLOMBE. O—oh! An R! *That's* who it is—that disgusting creature!

JULIEN. No—it's not a P *or* an R.

COLOMBE. It's not a W? Low as he is, I don't think, because a woman refused him, he'd do a thing like this!

JULIEN. No, Colombe, it's not a W.

COLOMBE. No. But if he's not the one—

JULIEN. What do you mean—if *he's* not the one?

COLOMBE. My poor boy, I can't even guess who it was—there's been one after another. They try to follow you into your dressing room, and you have to slam the door. They grab hold of you in the corridor and you have to slap their face. What do you think happens to a halfway attractive girl when men know she's alone?

JULIEN. *(Shouting)* I want their names— I want every one of their names!

COLOMBE. My poor darling, you'd need the telephone book.

(He sits on bench.)

Men are men—don't act so surprised, I'm sure you're no different.

JULIEN. Since I met you, I've never looked at another girl.

COLOMBE. Oh, of course not—you wouldn't dream of it.—What about the Chenaud twins, when you were teaching them waltzes for four hands.

JULIEN. They were fifteen years old!

COLOMBE. Precisely. The dark one was nothing much, I admit—but the other, with her silly child-like manner and firm mature breasts. You were always leaning over to show her the correct *(Pokes his chest)* position for the fourth finger. I dare you to deny it—I've received letters, too, in my day—only I didn't say anything.

JULIEN. The Chenaud kids—it's insane.

COLOMBE. And the druggist's wife?

JULIEN. The druggist's wife?

COLOMBE. Yes, my pet, the druggist's wife. You'd never go on an errand except when we had to have tooth powder or soap—and when we were broke, that tightwad, who'd skim milk at both ends if she could, would give *you* credit!—I'll give you credit, too—you had quite a way with her.—And to—to say these things to me— I'm not joking, Julien, I think you're awful. *(She starts to cry a second time.)*

(JULIEN *sits silent, at a loss for what to do. In the corridor, they feel that things may be straightening out and something had better be done. With pantomime, they persuade the* HAIRDRESSER *to go in. He knocks and half-opens the door.)*

HAIRDRESSER. They're going to ring up, Madame. Shall I run the comb through your hair once or twice?
COLOMBE. *(In tears)* Oh thanks, Lucien—yes, I need it.

(JULIEN *begins getting suspicious again when the* HAIRDRESSER *comes in: stands up, looks them over suspiciously while* HAIRDRESSER *works on* COLOMBE.)

(Smiling into the mirror) You're a nice man, Lucien— you try to make women pretty.
HAIRDRESSER. You're always pretty to begin with. Doing your hair's not work, it's a pleasure.
JULIEN. See here, my friend!

(HAIRDRESSER *turns around, comb in mid-air.)*
How long does it take to "run the comb through her hair once or twice"?
HAIRDRESSER. It depends, Monsieur Julien.
JULIEN. Depends on what?—And the comb's not enough; it also requires your hands, I see.
HAIRDRESSER. You can't comb curls.
JULIEN. Get out of here—or I'll run more than a comb—through more than your hair. Out! *(Pushes him out to corridor. Comes back, shouts)* He's not the one.
COLOMBE. He?
JULIEN. He couldn't be your lover. His hands are

like dough. How can you let him touch you? *(Shouts)* Answer me, Colombe, before I start a scene: it's not him?

COLOMBE. *(Getting up with a cry)* I know who wrote to you! It's not true when you say it's a man. All these hysterics because a drunken old bat saw me having dinner with the hairdresser.

JULIEN. *(Springing up)* You had dinner with him?

COLOMBE. I do have to eat, you know. Am I supposed to fast because you're in the army?

(In the corridor the HAIRDRESSER is very much annoyed; the OTHERS make fun of him.)

JULIEN. That baboon had the nerve to ask you to dinner—and you actually went? I'll—beat his brains out.

(Runs toward the door. The HAIRDRESSER pushes through the crowd, away from the door. COLOMBE catches hold of JULIEN.)

COLOMBE. Darling, you're behaving like a child. He's a greasy half-wit who never opens his mouth. Do you think if I wanted a lover I'd pick anything like that? Show a little sense!

JULIEN. He's not very pretty, is he?

COLOMBE. *(Laughs, kisses him)* My great big dope of a husband! I have him do my hair because he's so good at it: but otherwise—really I prefer you. *(Takes his hands, kisses him again)* Instead of fighting with me ever since you came, couldn't you once take me in your arms? *(She melts into his arms, locks his hands behind her, offers her lips.)*

JULIEN. *(Weakly)* But who is it then?

COLOMBE. It's no one, you silly. No, there is somebody— I'd better confess. It's you. *(She kisses him.)*

JULIEN. *(In her arms)* I love you, darling, and I'm so miserable. It'd be better to tell me if you've done something wrong. Don't you think I know how tough it is to be all alone? And in this filthy atmosphere. I'll get you out of it and we'll be happy again.

COLOMBE. *(Caressing him: genuinely tender)* My sweet foolish baby, who frightens everybody and is more defenseless than all the others—you're a brave man just the same.

JULIEN. *(Groaning, while she caresses him)* But how could you let them come near you—that fool that calls you his little monkey—

COLOMBE. Gaulois?

(Guffaws in the corridor.)

Fool is right! He thinks he's irresistible because he was good-looking thirty years ago. So he mumbles and whispers and tries to look passionate—

(In the corridor GAULOIS is very upset and amid guffaws goes into his room.)

JULIEN. And you let him—

COLOMBE. Yes, I let him—talk. That's all he *can* do. "My little monkey," and "my little mousie," and "I can't sleep for love," and "I can't eat for love"—and I'm sure he can't love for love, either. Pats your hand and then hurries home exhausted and takes off his corset and drinks his cocoa and sinks into bed. And he's in raptures because he has the strength to get up by noon the next day—and strap on, and lace on, and buckle on, and hammer on all his orthopedic appliances —and come back here and try to hold hands with one of the other girls. You think I need *that*— *(Putting arms around him)* when I have you?

JULIEN. But what did he mumble and whisper about?

COLOMBE. Well—that I should rehearse with him at his apartment—all done up in what he calls Moroccan style.

JULIEN. *(Pushing her away)* And you went?

COLOMBE. *(Upset)* No, darling-- Yes, once: but not alone. With Poet-Mine-Own, to run through a scene.

JULIEN. You see, the letter I got was true. You do go around with them, you do go to their apartments—

COLOMBE. But I told you: I went with Poet-Mine-Own, in his carriage.

JULIEN. *(Wounded once more; shouting)* But then you were alone with *him!*

COLOMBE. *(Exasperated, trying to be patient)* But I took him along so I wouldn't be alone with Gaulois.—Really, Julien, I couldn't bring someone else along so I wouldn't be alone with *him*.

JULIEN. Remember how Mine-Own behaved two years ago: I had to teach him manners.

COLOMBE. You were a very good teacher! Now he's courtly, but very well-behaved.

JULIEN. Courtly: and you let him be: you let him pay you court. Robinet—a man like that has juicy little parts to hand out. So we let him kiss the back of our gloves—and then stroke the back of our arm—and then—it's really very little, considering what you'll get out of it. Too bad he's got a tic; but you can stand it, can't you? Well, I can't! I've a little courting to do, too, with that old— *(Starts wildly for the door.)*

(Consternation in the corridor. COLOMBE *grabs him, while breaking into laughter.)*

COLOMBE. Darling—this is insane. Really it is!

JULIEN. What's so funny?—Because I'm ashamed? Because I'm upset?

COLOMBE. No, no! What you say—that he has a tic. Every time he gets excited? Can you imagine me in the arms of Poet-Mine-Own? Julien—just think of him in his underdrawers! *(She starts to laugh again: slowly her laughter wins him over.)*

JULIEN. I must admit that Mine-Own in under-drawers would be quite a sight!

COLOMBE. *(Laughing more)* You don't know the best part of it! He wears baby pink garters that his wife embroid— *(She turns away, laughing more.)*

JULIEN. *(Stops laughing, then she stops, terrified)* How would you know?

COLOMBE. *(Regaining her laugh)* Everyone does.

JULIEN. How do *you* know?

COLOMBE. *(Turns to him)* Deschamps told me.

JULIEN. Deschamps? That's the kind of thing you discuss with Deschamps! When was this?

COLOMBE. If you let me, I'll explain.

JULIEN. Don't tell me you went to his office—sat on the green divan where he gets reimbursed for handing out parts?

COLOMBE. No—well yes, once. Please let me explain, Julien: when I signed my contract. *(After a second)* All right, if you *must* know. He didn't make me any exception to what he does. I stopped him— I slapped his face. I told him what I thought he behaved like— and what I thought he looked like, too. Then I s'pose for fear Poet-Mine-Own might have a little better luck, he told me what *he* looked like—garters, and a few other details. Darling, that's all there was to it!

(The LIGHT in the corridor comes up brighter.)

JULIEN. *(Suddenly slapping her face: shouts)* Just a tramp, like all the rest. God damn you!

(COLOMBE *falls down in a faint.* JULIEN *rushes toward the door.* MME. ALEXANDRA, *dressed as a Marechale, who had come out of her dressing room to listen with the* OTHERS, *pushes them all aside and when* JULIEN *opens the door, she stands directly in front of him.)*

MME. ALEXANDRA. *(In her most terrible voice)* Well, sir?

JULIEN. Let me through— I want to see—

MME. ALEXANDRA. *(Blocking him)* Must you mess things up wherever you go? Do you always have to scream and start trouble? I felt sorry for you and took in your wife: now you get out of here and leave us alone.

JULIEN. It's you— *(To the* CROWD) —it's you who did this to her. *(To his mother)* And you, looking like a— I can't say what you remind me of. God damn you all!

MME. ALEXANDRA. *(Like thunder)* Stop that! I'm your mother.

JULIEN. Yes, you're my mother. Who'd know better than I?

MME. ALEXANDRA. You think I care for it? If it's not money, it's scenes. You let this child alone—she was just beginning to enjoy herself. She's supposed to lock herself up for life because you had the good taste to fall in love with her? Women will stick—if there's something to stick to! *(To* GOURETTE) Ring up! And Georgie, get that child on stage dead or alive!

(MME. GEORGES *glides into the dressing room to look after* COLOMBE.)

The audience is already making a commotion on account of this half-wit!

(She exits grandly up Center, her cane tapping in rhythm. Having parted to let her pass, the OTHERS *follow, while the BELL sounds and* GOURETTE *yelps.)*

GOURETTE. On stage for Act One! One stage for Act One!

COLOMBE. *(At this* COLOMBE *miraculously revives: looks in the mirror)* Is my hair all right?

MME. GEORGES. *(Getting costume from alcove)* It's fine, dear. Come along, I'll put your dress on downstairs.

(They run out up Center. The corridor LIGHT dims down to a glow. Everyone has gone, leaving all doors open. JULIEN *is alone, half-paralyzed, in the deserted corridor. Slowly he goes into* COLOMBE'S *room, looks around for a while, then*

*sits on pouf, head in hands. Below, the three TAPS
are heard and the orchestra begins the overture to
the "Realm of Passion." After a minute* EDOUARD
*appears down Left—walking jauntily in time with
the music and carrying a tiny bouquet. He goes
into* COLOMBE'S *dressing room, stops in surprise
on seeing* JULIEN *and doesn't know what to do
with the bouquet.)*

JULIEN. *(Looks at him: suddenly in a stunned tone)*
It's you.

EDOUARD. It's me all right.

JULIEN. *(This time in a sad voice)* It's you— I know
it's you.

EDOUARD. *(Looking quizzical, putting hat on bench)*
Sorry— I don't guess I know the combination. *(Nervously)* I'd have thought you'd be glad to see me. You
look fine.

JULIEN. Yes— I look fine.

EDOUARD. Army life not too hard?

JULIEN. Damn hard.

EDOUARD. *(Still trying to be casual)* Your feet holding out? When they go, everything goes. *(Tries to
laugh, but stops, seeing* JULIEN'S *face.)*

JULIEN. *(Gets up)* You're feeling chipper?

EDOUARD. *(Suddenly very much upset)* No.

(For a moment they stand silent, face to face.)

JULIEN. *(Moving away to Right)* Why did it have
to be you?

EDOUARD. *(Sits on bench. Quietly after a moment)*
What can you expect? You know what it's like around
here.

JULIEN. *(Shouting; turning on him)* No, I don't
know what it's like— I'll never know what it's like!

EDOUARD. *(Lowering his head)* No, I guess you
won't. You're different: you always were; even as a
kid, you fought against it. I couldn't, even as a kid—

when it only meant chocolates. It's always been that way. Enjoyment ahead of everything else. I'm scum.

JULIEN. Yes.

EDOUARD. What are you going to do?

(JULIEN *doesn't move.*)

(Loudly, as he gets up) Hit me—hard—hurt me. I want you to. You ought to have done it oftener when we were kids.

JULIEN. *(Choked)* No. Not you— I can't hurt you. *(Turns away)* I just want to know why. I can't understand.

EDOUARD. *(Going to him)* How can you understand our kind of life? We're not for you. All these slimy little male and female games—you'd never understand. Sock me, hard as you can: that's so much simpler—we'd be two little boys again. *(Putting flowers on table)* I can't ever say no, but this time I realized I'd have to get what was coming to me— I even want to get it.

JULIEN. No. I can't.

EDOUARD. *(Moving away, suddenly)* The little slut.

JULIEN. *(Hollowly)* Quit that.

EDOUARD. You think she acted right? I'm not defending myself, I'm damn weak. But she—she knew how you loved her—

JULIEN. *(Making a terrible effort)* God damn you, stop that!

EDOUARD. She had you, she had something—solid. And the first guy that fussed over her a little—he didn't even have to try hard.—You're lucky, to be above all this.

JULIEN. Yes. Just look at me.

EDOUARD. *(Taking him literally)* I can't— I'm too ashamed.

JULIEN. *(Suddenly)* I said to look at me.

EDOUARD. *(Turning away)* Sock me if you want—but I can't.

JULIEN. *(Forcing him)* I said look at me!

(EDOUARD *raises his eyes.*)

What's it all about?—a good enough nose, but what

the hell? A pretty little girl's weak mouth. The eyes of a drunk—the look of a baby-faced dissipated old man.

EDOUARD. You think I'm proud of it?—But you live off in space somewhere, you don't know what life is.

JULIEN. (Moving away) I'm beginning to find out.

EDOUARD. (Trying to regain his poise) You'd do better to go back to camp and forget about us all. At bottom you really want a hard life—something you can feel resentful about.

JULIEN. You're not even very clever with those cheap pearls of wisdom you pick up in club bars. I don't think you've ever been really moved in your life.

EDOUARD. That's not true. I've got just as much heart as you have. Only—

JULIEN. Only it's still wrapped in tissue paper in the box it came in.—If you'd had an air about you—but you even *dress* like a—jockey. (Loudly) Why? In Christ's name, why?

EDOUARD. Exactly. You dope women out!

JULIEN. (Shouting) I've got to find out! I've got to know what Colombe— Kiss me.

EDOUARD. (Embracing him, tears coming to his eyes) You mean you'll forgive me? Julien—

JULIEN. (Harshly holding on to him) Not that kind of kiss—the kind you gave *her!*

EDOUARD. (Trying to break away) Have you gone crazy? For God's sake, let me go.

JULIEN. (Yelling, struggling with him) Kiss me. Exactly the way you did her. I've got to know what she saw in you.

EDOUARD. (Struggling) My God, Julien—you're losing your mind. Let me go!

JULIEN. (Catching him by the throat) Kiss me, you stinking lousy bastard, the way you did her!

EDOUARD. (Choking) You're choking me.—Julien, I can't.

JULIEN. The way you did her. You could, once. Go on, pretend it's her. (He holds EDOUARD against himself.)

EDOUARD. *(Struggling again)* I can't. Oh!

*(*JULIEN *has set his mouth for a second against* EDOUARD'S: *then pushes him brutally away.* EDOUARD, *gasping, falls into a chair.* JULIEN *doesn't move: looks around searchingly, with a tormented face. Suddenly he wipes his mouth in disgust against the back of his hand.)*

JULIEN. *(In a voice of despair)* Colombe: I don't understand.

FAST CURTAIN

ACT TWO

SCENE II

The Curtain is then on the final scene of "The Realm of Passion." Louis XV decor as conceived around 1900. A salon with French windows opening upon a terrace. Beyond that, a Watteau-like park. The salon faces Right. The terrace and garden are at Left. Down Left, behind the salon, a small work bench. Up Center behind the salon, an upright piano and bench. Inside the salon, a couch Right of Center. Up Right a tall screen. A door up Right of Center. Another door down Center. "Off stage" MME. GEORGES *is sitting on the bench playing solitaire. Behind the down Center door,* GOURETTE *is pacing and studying his lines. Down Left a couple in costume are flirting. Up Center, two* STAGEHANDS *are reading newspapers. "On stage" at rise,* MME. ALEXANDRA *is Right of couch;* GAULOIS *below it.*

MME. ALEXANDRA.
Too long my lips were sealed, my heart on fire.

Now come, sweet youth, come swooning to my arms.
I am, like you, nineteen; I whisper, "Yes."
    GAULOIS. High lady, is it you?
    MME. ALEXANDRA.
'Tis I, indeed!
My young love opens to the fragrant night:
Erst I have never dared: tonight is elsewise!
Long in a golden cage my heart has paced
On fire but frustrate: now it melts the bars,
The fire mounts and love is himself aflame!
    GAULOIS. *(Sitting on couch)* My star!
    MME. ALEXANDRA. *(With a gesture of receding modesty)*
And now blot out my exalted rank!
Tonight no grande dame, but the maiden clay
Your hand shall mold, the white and quivering flesh
Your flesh shall warm! Yours only, yours to take.
    GAULOIS. *(Getting up with much personal difficulty, and pressing himself madly against her)*
Mine, mine forever, forever sweetly mine!
    MME. ALEXANDRA.
Moments there are milenniums cannot match!
    GAULOIS. *(Going to his knees)*

(TRUMPET calls in the distance.)

MME. ALEXANDRA. *(Suddenly crying out)*
Quick, off your knees, sweet boy! Quick for he comes!

(Followed by TWO TORCHBEARERS, GOURETTE appears, down Center, playing the Marechale De Villardiers. Perruke, plumed tricorne. hunting boots. whip. COLOMBE has come in, terrified, through another door, up Right of Center, and stations herself humbly near MME. ALEXANDRA.)

    GOURETTE.
O hateful sight! Oh heinous treachery!
Monsieur de Bouglaire kneeling at her feet!

MME. ALEXANDRA. *(Like a Racine heroine)*
Monsieur the Marshal of France, I love this boy!
(Goes and stands between the men.)
   GOURETTE. *(Grand and terrible, hand on sword)*
Wrath such as mine could cost your swain his life!
   GAULOIS.
Yours to decree, Monsieur the Marshal of France!
   GOURETTE. *(Moving up above sofa. With a smile at
once noble, wistful and profligate)*
I envy this boy's youth, I crave his ardor—
My royal master does not wish the sword
A Marshal wears to avenge such injury:
Our swords, Monsieur, must serve a nobler cause:
Post have I all night sped here from Versailles:
War is declared!

        (MME. ALEXANDRA moves down Center.)

   GAULOIS. *(Drawing himself erect, hand on sword)*
War, sir?
   GOURETTE.
Gallantry,
My gallant, moves from a lady's couch
To the river Rhine, to save our glorious France!
   GAULOIS. *(Drawing his sword; piously)*
Dear France!

        (TRUMPET calls in the distance.)

   GOURETTE.
Yes—one name we can both adore
With never a thought of doing each other hurt.
(Turns to MME. ALEXANDRA)
O chide him not Marie, if France he choose—
She is the fiercer mistress—but our Mother!
   MME. ALEXANDRA. *(Heartbroken but excessively
noble)*
Go both of you and leave me to my tears:
So fair a rival I too must wish should win.
   GOURETTE. *(Becoming very human)*

I know how so you suffer:
I too have loved. Loved *YOU*, Madame!—Alas!
(Kisses her hand)
Adieu!
(To GAULOIS*)* Monsieur!
   GAULOIS. *(With a helpless gesture, to* MME. ALEX-
ANDRA*)* Adieu!

(Amid a blare of TRUMPETS, he follows GOURETTE
   out the down Center door; MME. ALEXANDRA *falls
   sobbing into* COLOMBE'S *arms.)*

   MME. ALEXANDRA. My gallant boy!
   COLOMBE. *(Trying to console her)*
He will return, Madame, still faithful to you!
   MME. ALEXANDRA. *(After a brief tearful reverie)*
He—yes! But I?
   COLOMBE. You?
   MME. ALEXANDRA.
I am young and fair:
Others will come tonight to pay me court—
And madness 'twere, to make love bide the morrow:
Women will die for Love—but not sit waiting!
    (Sounds of a MINUET in the Park: TWO
    MASKED DANCERS *whirl across up Left of Center.)*
Clorinda, let us dance! Come, let's away:
The fiddles sing their love songs by the fountains;
Masked figures haunt the shrubbery: Come, sweet child
I'm nineteen— I'm a woman— I'm bewitched!
Come, let us blend the violet with the rose,
And swooning in Love's arms, forget Love's woes!

*(While MUSIC is heard offstage and there is dancing
   far upstage, they exit Left Center as fast as* MME.
   ALEXANDRA'S *robes will permit.)*

CURTAIN AT RIGHT CLOSES

(Frantic applause off Right. Curtain is drawn; EVERY-
ONE *takes bows.* MME. ALEXANRA *and* GAULOIS
are recalled several times; she yielding the stage

*to him, then coming on alone to be cheered. She
receives flowers; is choked with gratutide, indicates how grateful she is to the rest of the cast;
then the Curtain closes for good. At once everybody's attitude changes:* MME. ALEXANRRA *tosses
her flowers to* MME. GEORGES, *who has hurried
over with* MME. ALEXANDRA'S *cane. She exits Left,
worn out.* GAULOIS *follows, taking off his wig
while exiting.)*

GAULOIS. God, they were a tough crowd tonight.

(Still in costume, but without his hat and rapier,
GOURETTE *helps the* STAGEHANDS *start to clear the
stage.* JULIEN *comes on and stops* COLOMBE, *down
Left. During their scene together, the LIGHTS
go out and the* STAGEHANDS *clear the stage; the
salon is folded and flown up. The screen is removed
leaving only the couch. Till the two of them are
left alone in semi-darkness.)*

JULIEN. I've been walking the streets all evening—
I've got to talk to you.
    COLOMBE. *(Moving a little)* I have to go up and
undress.
    JULIEN. *(Blocking her)* Not, not up there. I can't
face them any more: I'm too ashamed.
    COLOMBE. All right, we'll stay here.
    JULIEN. I've seen Edouard.
    COLOMBE. *(Without expression)* Yes.
    JULIEN. He told me. You've seen him, too?
    COLOMBE. Yes.
    JULIEN. *(Going to couch)* You realize it was all the
harder to take because it was him.
    COLOMBE. *(In a composed little voice, coming to
Center)* Of course I do. I'm terribly sorry. We'd both
have given anything to spare you this.
    JULIEN. Ever since we were little boys he's taken
things from me; he can't help it. And now—you're *both*

young and pleasure-loving, and I left you here alone. And I realize that I lectured you too much, I got on your nerves, I guess.

COLOMBE. Yes.

JULIEN. The whole time I was walking the streets, I kept talking to you out loud. I explained everything to you. People stared at me. I'd bump into them and say, "Sorry" and walk on. Funny how you can walk and smile and keep saying "Sorry" when all the time you're dead. *(Silence)* You know, being dead makes you a lot easier on people. I want to forgive you, I really do: only first I want to understand.

COLOMBE. *(Has listened patiently; suddenly she speaks in a very calm way)* Baby, it would take a terribly long time to explain. And I'm petrified I'll be late. Don't you want to come up to my dressing room so we can talk while I get dressed?

JULIEN. *(Loudly)* Late? Late for what?

COLOMBE. *(Quietly)* For the supper date I told you about.

JULIEN. *(Not wanting to believe her)* After what's happened, you don't mean you're going to keep your date? I go back to camp tomorrow.

COLOMBE. I told you what it can mean to my future.

JULIEN. Are you out of your mind?

COLOMBE. It's you who won't understand. Why do we have to stay here—we could talk just as well upstairs. They'll be calling for me any minute.

JULIEN. After all that's happened between us, you're able to leave me and go out and enjoy yourself with a bunch of strangers!

COLOMBE. I'm not going with them to enjoy myself. I told you why I'm going. I'm thinking of my future.

JULIEN. Your future! *(Moving below couch)* It's quite different from your past: in the old days, if we fought, you were always very sweet to me afterwards.

COLOMBE. *(Coming to couch)* I want to be sweet now: I understand. But you ought to understand, too.

JULIEN. *(Looking at her)* It's just not possible. You

can't have stopped loving me. This thing between us is going to fester. We've got to stop it right away. You've been foolish, but we've still an awful lot to fall back on. *(After a moment, almost with shame)* We have the baby.

COLOMBE. *(Annoyed)* I was waiting for you to bring that up.

JULIEN. *(Turning away)* Wasn't it natural?

COLOMBE. Sure. It's very easy for you to get sentimental about the baby. But right now someone I'm paying with what I make is looking after him. And tomorrow morning it'll be me who wakes him up and bathes him and dries him off and gets his breakfast. That's what he's interested in, not what goes on between us. When he's older, I'll tell him how unhappy you made me, and that one day I couldn't take it any more.

JULIEN. *(Turning to her)* I made you unhappy?

COLOMBE. Yes.

JULIEN. But I did everything I knew how.

COLOMBE. Yes, everything you liked. You liked to stay home, so we never went out. I was so young and unsure about everything and you carefully explained what was right and what was wrong, so I used to say yes. But I really wanted to go dancing.

JULIEN. *(Sitting on couch)* We *went* dancing.

COLOMBE. Twice in two years. And if anyone else asked me to dance, you made me refuse.

JULIEN. But you said you loved me—

COLOMBE. *(Sitting beside him)* Couldn't I love you and also want to go dancing?

JULIEN. I never dreamt you wanted to!

COLOMBE. Of course you didn't! You thought I'd much rather stay home and hear your lectures on morality and how stupid people can be—or you played Beethoven by the hour, when if even for a minute I listened to a street singer with a guitar, you'd hurry over and slam down the window.

JULIEN. *(Getting up)* But I wanted you to like what was—beautiful.

COLOMBE. *(Getting up)* Who were you to decide what was beautiful? Things are beautiful if you love them, and I loved gypsy music and dancing and pretty clothes. But you never tried to find out what I might want, never asked me anything, never bought me anything.

JULIEN. *(Going below to Left of Center)* We hadn't any money.

COLOMBE. And you couldn't be bothered to make any. All that mattered was your becoming a great pianist. And so that you could become a great pianist, I had to wash dishes and scrub floors. And if you'd ever become one, while you stood bowing and drinking in the applause, I'd have had my beautiful red hands to show the public.

JULIEN. Please don't—this is awful.

COLOMBE. It *is* awful. But it's over. I support myself now, I live the way I like. When something amuses me I laugh without worrying whether you'll think it's funny, or start to sulk as soon as we get home.

JULIEN. *(Turning to her)* If I sulked it was because it hurt me to see you suddenly do the kind of things that—

COLOMBE. *(Going to him)* Well, I won't hurt you after this. We've both suffered plenty from your always being hurt. It's good to be sensitive but really, Julien, there are limits. Would you like me to be honest? I've been very happy since you went away. When I wake up the sun's shining, I look out the window and for the first time in years there's no tragedy in the street.

(He moves away and sits on bench down Left.)
And if the mailman rings and I go to the door in my nightgown—there's no drama. I'm not a loose woman—we're just a young girl and the mailman, happy with each other—he because he gets a kick out of seeing me in a nightgown, I because I've given him a little pleasure. I like the whole business—being attractive and nib-

bling breakfast while I do the house work, and washing myself in the kitchen, naked, with the window open. And if the old man opposite runs for his opera glasses, I can't get excited, or feel I'm a loose woman and cry for two hours trying to calm you down. You'll never know, my darling, how uncomplicated life can be—without you.

JULIEN. But if I was jealous and made scenes, it was because I loved you. So would any other man.

COLOMBE. No. Or if he does, I'll have sense enough now to laugh.

JULIEN. Edouard doesn't love you—you know he doesn't.

COLOMBE. *(Moving away a little)* I know he doesn't love me the way one dreams of being loved. But he makes me happy and that's a lot. He tells me I'm beautiful and brings me little presents and takes care of me.

JULIEN. *(Getting up and going above bench)* Me! Me! That's all you know how to say.

COLOMBE. *(Turning to him)* Yes, I've learned. I heard the word often enough from you.

JULIEN. *(Turning away)* I'm hurt, Colombe.

COLOMBE. It's very sad. But I was hurt, too.

JULIEN. *(Turning to her)* But I never meant to hurt you—whatever I did, it was because I loved you.

COLOMBE. No, Julien—because you loved yourself.

JULIEN. *(Turning away)* That's nonsense.

COLOMBE. *(Going to him)* The girl you loved was something you dreamt up. I want the next man to love *me* and I want loving me to make him happy. It never made you happy. You'll never understand women—but that's all they know how to do in the world—make men happy. You shouldn't cheat them out of it.—Now I'll be late. We've said everything: let me go and get ready.

JULIEN. *(Grabbing her by the wrist)* No.

COLOMBE. Let me go.

JULIEN. No.

COLOMBE. You're hurting me, Julien.—Go ahead, you

know how. Slap my face. It won't be the first time tonight.

(They struggle and fall on couch. While they've been speaking, the props and furniture have been removed, one by one, leaving only the couch. The STAGEHANDS *come up to them.)*

STAGEHAND. Mr. Julien, we've got to move this, too.

*(*JULIEN *gets up without a word; the men take the couch and put it to one side—place piano and bench Right of Center, then remove couch off Left.* JULIEN *has drawn* COLOMBE *to him down Left. They're alone and face to face, on a big empty stage lighted only by a work lamp.)*

JULIEN. We're crazy to yell at each other. I'm going to talk to you very quietly: will you listen?

COLOMBE. No.

JULIEN. *(Grabbing her wrist)* You're going to have to!

COLOMBE. You're stronger than I am: you can even kill me if you feel like it. The poor wronged husband— I'm sure they'd acquit you.

JULIEN. I only want to ask one thing. Will you promise to answer?

COLOMBE. It all depends. What is it?

JULIEN. When I came into your dressing room a while ago, why did you throw your arms around me?

COLOMBE. Because I was so glad to see you. I mean it.

JULIEN. And then when I questioned you, when I suspected the others, why did you deny it as though you'd never even kissed another man?

COLOMBE. Imagine being suspicious of those characters— But I'd never have admitted it about anybody. It could only make things worse. I love you; you have to go back to camp tomorrow. This was no time to upset you.

JULIEN. And if I hadn't seen Edouard, and *had*

believed you? You'd have come back from this supper
date and got into bed with me?

COLOMBE. Yes.

JULIEN. And given yourself to me?

COLOMBE. *(In a small even voice)* Of course.

JULIEN. *(Sitting on bench, facing up stage. After a
silence)* I don't understand.

COLOMBE. *(Standing above him)* You never understand anything! I love you—that's all. You're all alone
in camp. You've just spent three months without a
woman— I know you haven't been unfaithful. If you
hadn't found out, do you think I'd have invented a
headache or something to spoil your leave? I'm not that
mean.

JULIEN. And you'd have gone through with it like
a street-walker, without any pleasure?

COLOMBE. *(Sincerely)* Why without any pleasure?
You give me a lot of pleasure.

JULIEN. And Edouard?

(A second.)

COLOMBE. *(Moving away to Center)* Yes. But that's
something else. *(Turns to him)* You have a real genius
for complicating everything.

JULIEN. And you'd have told him about it?

COLOMBE. *(Indignant)* Of course not! What business is it of his? Edouard hasn't any rights over me.
(Going to him) Look, I've never let him say one word
against you. What do you think I am?

(Silence. JULIEN, *stunned, dares not answer.)*
(Softly) Baby, you'll let me go and get dressed now?
I promise I won't stay at Maxim's long: I'll come home
to you as fast as I can.

JULIEN. *(As though questioning himself)* We really
still love each other—at any rate, this way?

COLOMBE. Yes.

JULIEN. I'm ashamed to ask—you never just pretended with me?

COLOMBE. No. Never.

JULIEN. *(Getting up and moving away to Center)* Then why? I just can't understand why. *(Turning to her)* Do you love Edouard more than me?

COLOMBE. No.

JULIEN. As much?

COLOMBE. Do you think I keep score? Could I go out with Edouard all the time, let him look after me, and then give him a kiss on the forehead and say "Run along now." *(Going to him)* *You've* got to make a little effort to understand, too.

JULIEN. *(Unhappily, moving away to down Right of Center)* I do— I don't do anything else.

COLOMBE. *(Following)* But *our* way—not just yours.

JULIEN. Then, if this leave hadn't turned up, you'd have gone on sharing the two of us?

COLOMBE. If— If. I don't live on *ifs. If* you'd stayed in Paris, this would never have happened. But you didn't: it's partly your fault. Don't always blame other people.

JULIEN. I had to go into service sometime, like everyone else.

COLOMBE. If you'd loved me, you could have got deferred. They said they could get you, and you refused. That's precisely when I realized that you think of no one but yourself *(Moving away to Left of Center)* and that I'd better start thinking of myself, too.

JULIEN. *(Suddenly tender)* My poor baby.

COLOMBE. Yes, your poor baby. *(Turning away)* And you're not making her look any prettier when she needs to!

JULIEN. *(Going to edge of piano)* My poor little baby —all she can think of is her supper date!—I loved you the way a little boy loves his mother, or loves another little boy when they prick each other's blood and swear eternal friendship. The way two people do who plan and struggle and worry together till they're old and, sitting side by side, start dreaming back. To love that way seemed all the romance a man could need : he could forget about the things he'd never done—forget about the girls you *don't* forget about.

COLOMBE. *(A little hurt, turning to him)* Now you can do them—and take the girls along. Ask them to go away with you, as you did me two years ago.

JULIEN. *(Turning away)* Yes, I could.

COLOMBE. I can see you bewitching them with your sad eyes and your beautiful wounded soul—what a little nit-wit I was!

JULIEN. *(Grabbing her wrist; loudly)* Don't run down the old Colombe ; at least *she's* still mine.

COLOMBE. Yours, my poor dodo? What did you know about her ? You thought she was a little angel ?— in a florist shop where a bunch of old bucks came day after day for their carnations ? And the funeral wreaths I'd take to grief-stricken households : but there was always a cousin who'd manage to control his grief and push you in a corner. Keep your little angel if it makes you happy : but there aren't any angels. Even if you want to be—

JULIEN. *(Grabbing her)* Damn you, I won't let you throw mud at that girl !

COLOMBE. *(In an I-will-if-I-feel-like-it tone)* It's me, after all !

JULIEN. No—it's not you! *(Looks at her with both pity and hate)* That's what scares me worst of all— that you could get to be so vile I'd stop loving you.

COLOMBE. *(Quietly)* You're hurting me, Julien—in a minute I'll be all black and blue. I can't see where that'll do us any good.

JULIEN. *(Suddenly letting her go)* All right—this time you can go. Hurry up, keep your date.

(She turns and walks Left without looking at him as soon as he has released her. He watches her go; suddenly cries.)

Colombe!

COLOMBE. *(Turning)* Now what?

JULIEN. *(Tormentedly)* Nothing— If while you're

dressing you decide to break your date, I'll be waiting
here.

*(With a slight shrug, she turns and exits Left. JULIEN
remains alone, disconsolate, in the middle of the
stage. Starts to go after COLOMBE, then pulls back,
stands nervously trying to make up his mind. As
he deliberates, MME. ALEXANDRA appears from
down Left bundled up in scarves and leaning on
a cane: after her comes MME. GEORGES carrying a
shopping bag.)*

*(Stage LIGHTS fade down except for a pool of light
around the piano.)*

JULIEN. *(Going to her)* Mother!
MME. ALEXANDRA. What do you mean—"Mother"?
Have you gone crazy? *(She moves away from him and
starts out Right.)*
JULIEN. *(Going after her)* Mother, I'm so unhappy.
MME. ALEXANDRA. *(Stops Right of piano and turns
to him)* You made your bed—now you'll have to lie in
it alone.
JULIEN. *(Sitting on piano bench)* Mother, I loved
her— I'll always love her.
MME. ALEXANDRA. Your father would have always
loved me. That's what made everything so impossible.
What is this mania to love someone all one's life? Why
should we? Do we always wear the same clothes? Do
we always live in the same house? Ask the doctor, he'll
tell you that there's not a cell in your body that was
there seven years before. Everything else about us
changes—why shouldn't our feelings change? These
romantic ideas you people pick up in books—they've
nothing to do with life. If your sensitive Colonel of a
father had started in the way I did, in a mangy old road
company at fourteen, he'd never have committed sui-
cide.—Let's go, Georgie. You haven't forgotten my
knee pad?

(Mme. Georges comes and stands above piano.)

Julien. *(Getting up and clinging to her)* But all the same you must have suffered. Nobody can reach your age and not suffer. There must be something we can say to each other: I feel so desperately lonely.

Mme. Alexandra. You'll always feel lonely. Always —because you never think of anyone but yourself. You think *I'm* the selfish one? The really selfish people aren't those who insist on having good times. They're not dangerous, they don't take any more than they give. They know only too well: they pass one another by, they pat one another's hand, you say hello to me, I say hello to you: we both know how little it means, but we can both put up a little better with what's gnawing inside us, what no one gives a damn about except ourselves. The dangerous ones are those who stop you every time you want to turn around, who instead of patting your hand, insist that you feel their guts. And the more they suffer, the more they make you suffer, the happier they are.

Julien. *(Sitting down again and groaning)* But I love her!

Mme. Alexandra. Yes, I guess that's true. But now she doesn't love you any more. That's just as true, that counts just as much. What's she supposed to do—be bored to death for the next sixty years because that's the one way to keep you happy?

Julien. I did everything I knew how—

Mme. Alexandra. Yes, but you didn't *know* how—and you never will. Go home and go to bed and tomorrow go back to being a soldier. Spill those guts of yours for France: she may thank you for them; we can't. *(Wincing with pain)* Let's go, Georgie—my knee's killing me from standing here. *(She hobbles toward the wings at Right. Suddenly calling out)* Was it money you wanted?

Julien. No, Mother—thank you.

MME. ALEXANDRA. Have it your own way.—Try to get some sense!

(She and MME. GEORGES *exit up Right.* JULIEN, *alone on the empty stage, turns to the piano, opens it, plays a few vague notes, stops. We hear far off a piano playing, over again, the music* JULIEN *has just stopped playing, and which proceeds melodically beyond where he has stopped.* JULIEN *cries out: "Colombe, don't you remember?—I remember." His head on the piano, he doesn't seem to hear. LIGHTS dim till it is dark: In the darkness the piano plays a waltz that comes nearer and seems real, as if played on stage. The work bench and railing are cleared. When the LIGHTS slowly come on again,* JULIEN *is in civilian clothes, and about to play the same piano. The stage is still empty and only lit by a work lamp, but sunlight streams through the air shafts. Then* COLOMBE *stands there in an old dress carrying a large florist's basket of flowers. She seems to have lost her bearings; suddenly catches sight of* JULIEN.*)

COLOMBE. *(Down Left of Center)* I'm sorry, Monsieur: Mme. Alexandra's dressing room?

JULIEN. It's up a flight. But why don't you wait here?—she'll be here any minute to rehearse. That'll save you a whole flight of steps and a tornado. She's all set to blow down the theatre.

COLOMBE. Is something wrong?

JULIEN. In the theatre, something's always wrong.

COLOMBE. She's such a wonderful actress—and isn't she beautiful?

JULIEN. Oh, very. Like an old public building.

COLOMBE. That's mean of you. And she's not old: I saw her act once.

JULIEN. That's different. On the stage she looks twenty.

COLOMBE. That's not very nice, seeing you work for her. What if she heard you?

JULIEN. *(Still at the piano)* She has. I'm her son.

COLOMBE. You're her son?

JULIEN. Uh hum. Not that either one of us boasts about it.

COLOMBE. Then, you see, she isn't old.

JULIEN. *(Smiling, and turning round on the piano stool)* Why?

COLOMBE. *(Stammering a little)* Because you're—so very young.

JULIEN. *(Blushing, and stammering, too)* I don't go in much for compliments—but you're terribly pretty.

(A sudden pained silence between them.)

Is it fun to be a florist?

COLOMBE. *(Coming a little closer)* Not always as much as it is today.

JULIEN. You must meet a lot of people.

COLOMBE. Yes, only it's mostly *old men* who buy flowers.

JULIEN. When I'm rich I'll buy some—and give them to you.

COLOMBE. Really?

JULIEN. Do people ever give you flowers?

COLOMBE. Never!

JULIEN. What about your boy friend?

COLOMBE. I don't have one.

JULIEN. *(Suddenly getting up and coming to clip a rose from the basket)* Here— I'll start in right now.

COLOMBE. Oh, the basket! This'll cause trouble.

JULIEN. I'll take care of it. There'll be trouble anyhow, just because I'm here.

COLOMBE. *(Smelling her rose)* Funny, when they're given to you, you feel like smelling them. Doesn't your mother like you to come to the theatre?

JULIEN. No.

COLOMBE. She's afraid you'll meet the wrong type of people?

JULIEN. *(Laughing)* That's marvelous! No: she's

afraid I'll ask her for money. I'm trying to be a con-
cert pianist and I practice eight hours a day: that
doesn't leave much time to earn a living. So sometimes
I have to come here for—supplies. As seldom as possible, because I hate the idea.

COLOMBE. It's good to have pride.

JULIEN. *(Sitting on piano bench)* It's also tough.

COLOMBE. *(Coming closer)* If I loved somebody, I'd
want him to have pride—to be a real man.

(They smile but don't know what to say next.)

JULIEN. Do you make lots of money as a florist?

COLOMBE. Oh, with tips about one hundred francs a
month.

JULIEN. Then you're in my class.—If—if I pick you
up after work some night, would you have dinner with
me?—you wouldn't insist on Larue?

COLOMBE. I wouldn't even know where it was. But
I once had dinner at Poccardi's.

JULIEN. *(Getting up and moving to Right)* Well,
we'll go there again.

COLOMBE. And eat up all the hors d'oeuvres?

JULIEN. Sure, and then yell for more.

COLOMBE. *(Going to him)* You really *will?*

JULIEN. I hereby *do.* Tonight. Why wait?

COLOMBE. You can't call for me at the shop tonight;
this was my last errand.

JULIEN. *(Takes her hand)* Wonderful: then we can
start off right now.

COLOMBE. But there's my basket.

JULIEN. *(Goes and puts basket on piano top)* Just
leave it here. It's big enough—they're sure to notice
it.

COLOMBE. *(Suddenly practical)* Do you think I
should wait for my tip?

JULIEN. I'm crazy: we both gotta wait for our tip.
We'd sure do well at Poccardi's on my twenty-one sous.

COLOMBE. *(Going to him)* I suppose you think I

always say yes—like this. But it's really the first time.

JULIEN. It's the first time I ever asked anyone.—Do you think it's possible?

COLOMBE. What?

JULIEN. That people can like each other—no, it's not just—like—can feel something about each other right away?

COLOMBE. I don't know.

JULIEN. *(Who has sat down next to her on piano bench, and puts his arm over her shoulder)* Do you feel that way?

COLOMBE. Yes.

JULIEN. Do you, very often?

COLOMBE. No.

JULIEN. I *never* have. I'd better tell you before we go out— I'm a dreadful person. I don't like people, I get infuriated at them—and they don't like me.

COLOMBE. I don't believe it.

JULIEN. It's true, though.

COLOMBE. You seem very nice to me.

JULIEN. You know— I find that I can be!—Ever go to the Zoo?

COLOMBE. Uh hum.

JULIEN. D'you ever watch the bears? I'm a bear. Think you'd like to tame me?

COLOMBE. *(Leaning against his shoulder)* They're strong. They protect you—and keep you warm. There's nothing wrong with bears.

JULIEN. Maybe not, but most girls don't like them.

COLOMBE. I'm not sure what I like; but right now I know I feel fine. The only thing that scares me is—it's all happening so fast.

JULIEN. I'm even more scared than you. I've waited all my life for a girl who likes bears.

COLOMBE. I'm glad.

JULIEN. If it were only true—if it could be like in fairy tales; at first sight, and then forevermore. Promise me you'll be faithful till tonight at any rate —till Poccardi's.

COLOMBE. I promise.

JULIEN. Cross your heart.

COLOMBE. *(Doing so)* Cross my heart.

JULIEN. *(Shyly)* Is it too soon to kiss you?

COLOMBE. *(Whispering)* No. *(Offers him her lips.)*

JULIEN. *(Kisses her, then suddenly stands up and cries out)* God, this is wonderful!— *(Moving to Left of Center)* Can life really be good? Is Mother really charming and young, after all? We've got to celebrate this. *(Takes the basket)* Here, why be stingy—take the rest.

COLOMBE. *(Running to him. Groaning)* But they were sent to your mother, Monsieur. *(Suddenly)* Monsieur what?

JULIEN. Julien. And you?

COLOMBE. Colombe.

JULIEN. *(Picking her up and swinging her around)* Mademoiselle Colombe! But what is happening tonight that makes life suddenly seem so wonderful?

(MADAME ALEXANDRA *rushes in up Right, followed by her staff:* MINE-OWN, DESCHAMPS, GOURETTE *and* MME. GEORGES.)

MME. ALEXANDRA. Slime! Those bit actors are all slime! And we open in three days. *(Sees* JULIEN *and stops)* What are you doing here? You're all we need!

JULIEN. Mother darling, as you see, I'm kissing the florist.

MME. ALEXANDRA. *(Not understanding)* What are you talking about? Gourette, take the flowers and give her ten sous.

(GOURETTE *gives* COLOMBE *money and hands flowers to* MME. GEORGES, *who stands up Left.* GOURETTE *goes and stands above piano.* JULIEN *goes up Left.)*

And Deschamps, could you have the kindness to arrange for a few auditions this evening?

DESCHAMPS. *(Down Right of Center)* But the little brunette who tried out this afternoon—

MME. ALEXANDRA. *(Sitting on piano bench)* The little brunette is chiefly able to wiggle.

DESCHAMPS. She's most unusual.

MINE-OWN. *(Down Right, who has been looking at* COLOMBE) We're all crazy—

(Going to COLOMBE, *who has moved away to down Right.)*

for two hours we've been wrangling—over what? A girl to play a little florist— *(Taking the frightened* COLOMBE *by the hand and presenting her)* Here is a little florist, and an enchanting one.

MME. ALEXANDRA. *(Inspecting her through a lorgnette)* She is nice. Let's see your legs.

COLOMBE. *(Flabbergasted)* My legs?

MME ALEXANDRA. Yes. You've never heard of legs before?

MINE-OWN. Come, little lady, show us your legs: they may make you famous.

(She lifts her skirts a little.)

They're adorable— *(Lifting them higher with his cane)* see for yourselves.

COLOMBE. *(Pulling down her skirt)* But, Monsieur—

MINE-OWN. A bit higher, just a tiny bit higher.

JULIEN. *(Coming forward between them and pulling down* COLOMBE'S *skirts)* Let this young lady alone!

MINE-OWN. But we've got to see her legs—they're part of the plot.

JULIEN. They're always part of the plot.

MME. ALEXANDRA. That will do, Julien. *(To the* OTHERS) I agree she has pretty legs. But she still needs to have a voice.

(JULIEN moves away up Left.)

DESCHAMPS. *(Assenting with a gesture)* Ever done anything in the theatre?

COLOMBE. No, Monsieur, I work in a flower shop.

MME. ALEXANDRA. Have you ever done any singing?
COLOMBE. For my own pleasure.
MME. ALEXANDRA. Do you know "Love is Gone"?
COLOMBE. Sort of.
MME. ALEXANDRA. *(Gets up)* We'll see. Julien!—
where is that oaf?
JULIEN. *(Coming down from his corner)* I'm here.

(MINE-OWN *moves away to down Left.*)

MME. ALEXANDRA. Go to the piano and accompany
this girl.
JULIEN. *(Without moving)* No.
MME. ALEXANDRA. What do you mean, no?
JULIEN. I've a badly infected finger.
MME. ALEXANDRA. Where's it infected?
JULIEN. It's *getting* infected.
MME. ALEXANDRA. Why won't you play?
JULIEN. Because I'm not in the mood. Because I
think you should leave this girl alone. She's happy
where she is. *(To* COLOMBE*)* Sing without any piano.

(To EDOUARD, *who has just come in down Right.)*
(JULIEN *goes up Left*) Edouard, can you play "Love
Is Gone" with one finger?

EDOUARD. *(Goes to piano)* I can play Haydn's *Crea-
tion* with one finger.

MME. ALEXANDRA. Then accompany this child: your
brother has refused to.

EDOUARD. All right, let her rip. *(Starts to play.)*

COLOMBE. *(At first very nervously, then quite nicely)*
        A leaf in the spring
        Will cling to the tree
        A leaf in the fall
        Will blow away.

        So love like the leaf
        Will cling to your heart
        Will sing at the start
        And then will vanish
        But life must still go on

(MINE-OWN *interrupts about here.*)

And even though love is gone
You'll find your tears
Will melt like snow when winter's
Through, spring is here—love is new.

So I'll try again, and I'll laugh again
I may cry again but I won't care
There's one thing I learn
From watching the leaves
They always return
To bloom tomorrow.

(MINE-OWN, *in rapture, makes gestures after every phrase: has never heard anything like it. After hovering around her, he puts his arm around her waist. She tries, while singing, to free herself. He won't let her go. Nobody notices this little struggle except* JULIEN, *who suddenly strides over, pushing the* OTHERS *aside, and pulls* MINE-OWN *away from* COLOMBE.)

JULIEN. That's enough!
  (COLOMBE *stops singing.*)
You stay away from her.
  MINE-OWN. Who put you in charge?
  JULIEN. This young lady is *with* me.
  MME. ALEXANDRA. You don't even belong here yourself!
  JULIEN. This young lady is with me.
  MME. ALEXANDRA. That will be your exit line! Etienne! Jacques!
  STAGEHANDS. *(Coming in from down Left)* Yes, Madame Alexandra?
  MME. ALEXANDRA. Escort this clown to the street.
  STAGEHANDS. Go on, Monsieur Julien. Say bye-bye.
  JULIEN. Keep your hands off me.

(They try to push him out; he fights them.)

STAGEHANDS. Get going, Monsieur Julien.—Hey!

COLOMBE. *(Terrified)* Stop that. Make them stop, they'll hurt him.

JULIEN. *(Has managed to get out of their clutches and starts running around the stage. Yelling)* Besides, before I leave, I've a duty to perform. *(Goes up to* MINE-OWN, *turns him around and kicks him in the pants)* I swing an adorable leg, too!

MINE-OWN. *(Hand on pants seat)* You—you've torn my trousers!

DESCHAMPS. *(Yelling at the same time)* Get him out of here!

(The STAGEHANDS *have taken hold of* JULIEN *and are starting to drag him out Left.)*

MME. ALEXANDRA. The girl's all right, I'll settle for her. We'll rehearse her after dinner.

MINE-OWN. *(Hurrying over to* COLOMBE, *after making sure* JULIEN *has been collared)* It means fame, my child. *(Whispers in her ear)* I'm wild about you.

JULIEN. *(Yelling as he is dragged off)* Let me go, you bastards! *(To* COLOMBE*)* Poccardi's? You said you would!

COLOMBE. *(Pulling away from* MINE-OWN*)* You're disgusting—all of you. *(To* JULIEN*)* I meant it! I'll go with you to Poccardi's.

MME. ALEXANDRA. *(Going below to Left)* What's all this crap about Poccardi's? You rehearse tonight!

COLOMBE. Yes. But before I got the job, I accepted an invitation to dinner.

MME. ALEXANDRA. *Oh?* Indeed! *(Turning abruptly to* DESCHAMPS*)* Go fetch your little brunette—if she's free for the evening. At least she won't act like Joan of Arc. *(Exits down Left in a rage.)*

*(*MINE-OWN *starts going after her.)*

DESCHAMPS. Thank you, dear lady. You'll see—she's most unusual. *(Exits down Right.)*

(JULIEN comes running back and goes to Right of COLOMBE.)

MINE-OWN. *(Approaching JULIEN stiffly)* Monsieur, two of my friends will wait upon you tomorrow.

JULIEN. Splendid. Though I fear they won't find me at home. *(Put his arm around COLOMBE)* We're both—vanishing tonight.

MINE-OWN. *(In a rage to COLOMBE)* You ridiculous little fool. *(Exits down Left as fast as dignity permits.)*

(JULIEN wants to go after him but COLOMBE prevents him.)

COLOMBE. *(Tenderly)* No.

JULIEN. Did you hear what he said?

COLOMBE. No, I'm too happy. I heard something much nicer.

EDOUARD. *(Who has stayed at the piano: smiling)* Well, my love-birds, that was quite a scene—you sure know how to bring down the curtain.—Have you known each other long?

JULIEN. An hour.

COLOMBE. Don't tell him—he won't believe it.

EDOUARD. *(Getting up)* You'd rather go to dinner at Poccardi's with this—crank than get started in the theatre? *(To JULIEN)* Where did you find such a marvel?

JULIEN. That's my secret.

EDOUARD. No, don't tell. *(To JULIEN)* I hope you're not planning to make her miserable—you're not going to deliver your famous series of lectures?

JULIEN. No.

EDOUARD. Be happy, my children!—And say, I had good luck for once last night—we'll go halves like brothers. *(Holds out money.)*

JULIEN. *(Taking the money and shaking hands)*
You're terribly kind, Edouard.

EDOUARD. *(About to exit Left)* Have fun! Have as
much fun as you can!

COLOMBE. Thank you, Monsieur.

(He goes out Left. JULIEN *follows a few steps. They
come back to each other. The stage LIGHTS go
down to a glow of blue light to follow spot.)*

JULIEN. *(Takes her hand)* Here we are. I'll always
remember what you just did.

COLOMBE. You mustn't feel that way— I didn't even
know I was doing it. I screamed,—didn't I, when they
started to put you out— It's happened too fast, hasn't
it—it can't be the real thing.

JULIEN. Terribly fast, but I think it *is* the real
thing—and for the rest of our lives.

(They kiss: she leans against him, murmurs.)

COLOMBE. My darling. The rest of our lives.

JULIEN. That's the very least—

COLOMBE. *(Pressing hard against him)* Always—-
(More softly) Always, always—

(They kiss and JULIEN *takes her hand.)*

JULIEN. Now the story begins!

*(They walk, arms behind each other's back, toward the
wings Left.)*

SLOW CURTAIN

MADEMOISELLE COLOMBE

MUSIC NOTE

For permission to use the music of "Love Is Gone" in the production of this play, please write to Mills Music, Inc., 1619 Broadway, New York, 19, N. Y., who publish it under the title of "No Regrets."

PROPERTY LIST

Backstage, Paris 1900

Alexandra's Dressing Room

Act I, Scene I

1 make-up table (elaborate with canopy) Left of Center
1 armchair (large, elaborate) Right of table
1 foot-stool (below armchair)
1 round pouf (15" diameter—Louis XV) down Right
1 rectangular pouf (24 x 12") above round pouf
1 4-fold screen (chinese-bamboo) against wall up Right
1 small chair—below screen
1 small table—Right of small chair
1 small armchair—against wall up Left above door
1 cheval mirror—on stand—down Left below door
1 tall basket of roses—below Center door leading into corridor
1 potted palm—behind screen—on pedestal
1 basket of flowers—on small table, up Center behind make-up table
1 basket of lilies—above cheval mirror
1 basket of flowers—up Left corner of room
1 large Persian rug—center of platform
2 small skins—on rug

On Make-up Table
1 gold handmirror
1 atomizer
3 bottles assorted perfumes
Assorted make-up powder, puffs, etc.,
2 head-forms—1 white wig—1 red wig
1 set of red curls in tissue paper
1 jewel box (containing: Spanish comb, diamond-studded—diamond ear-rings, diamond choker)
2 brackets (practical—on table mirror)

On Small Table. Below screen
Small statue of woman (translucent, wired for light)
Sewing basket and blouse (on shelf of table)

On Walls
Mask of a woman
2 colored feathers and two fans
2 pictures of actresses
Bronze wreath

On Stage Left. Backing
3 small pictures

Off Left
Assorted—letters, bills, pencil (Gourette)

In Corridor
1 small chair—down Right
1 small stool—off Right
1 bracket—on Right wall (practical)

Note:
Two small 4-candle chandeliers, 1—down Right of Center; 1 down Left of Center hang throughout the show.

Act I, Scene II—Empty Stage
1 round table (24" diameter, with center leg) down Left

1 armchair, cane back—Right of table
1 small chair, Left of table
1 deck playing cards, on table
1 prop tree (with grass base) up Right of Center

Off Right
Pad and pencil (Gourette)
Manuscript (Edouard)

Off Left
"Goddess" robe (Mme. Georges)

Colombe's Dressing Room

Act II, Scene 1
1 make-up table, with mirror, against Right wall
1 square pouf, Left of table
1 closet, down Right (containing two dresses)
1 3-fold screen, up Left in front of alcove
1 small bench, (30"—below screen)
2 pieces of assorted woman's underwear, on clothes
   line in alcove
Colombe's 'play-within-the-play' costume, in alcove
2 brackets (practical) on table mirror

On Table
Assorted make-up sticks
Large powder-puff and container—jar of lip rouge
Small atomizer, comb and brush
Small hand mirror
2 small bottles of perfume
White handkerchief

On Walls
2 Chinese fans
2 ostrich feathers
1 mask of a woman

Off Right
1 small nosegay of flowers (Edouard)
Baton or tall marechal's stick (Alexandra) 6' white
   and gold

In Corridor
1 chair, on platform—down **Left at railing**
1 bracket (practical)

Stage "The Realm of Passion"
"Play-Within-The-Play"

Act II, Scene II
4-fold screen (18th Century design) up **Right**
Sofa-couch (18th Century gold satin) down **Right of**
Center
3-fold flat—with door up Right ⎤
French window Center   ⎬ Scenery
Door down Left of Center   ⎦
Small balcony rail—down **Left**
Small work bench—36" long—down **Left of Center**
Deck of cards—on bench.
Alexandra's cane—on bench
Upright piano (practical) up **Center**
Piano bench—on top of piano
French newspaper—on piano

Off Right
1 basket of assorted flowers (with **2 sprigs of roses,**
detachable) (Colombe)
1 sheet of music manuscript ⎤
1 pencil   ⎬ (Julien)
1 bouquet of roses   ⎦

MADEMOISELLE COLOMBE

COSTUME PLOT

ACT I—SCENE I

COLOMBE
(1st costume)

Street dress—orchid
Small hat—orchid
Shoes, gloves, purse—black

(2nd costume)

Blue costume ('Rosalind')
Small flower head dress

MME. ALEXANDRA
(1st costume)

Street dress—dark blue
Shawl—maroon
Purse, shoes—black
Large hat—black with green feathers
Red wig—cane—costume jewelry

(2nd costume)

Robe—red with black lace
Gloves—dark blue

JULIEN
Street suit—black cordoroy
Blue shirt—white collar—black tie
Black shoes

MME. GEORGES
Dark brown dress—black apron
Black shoes—knitted maroon shawl

POET-MINE-OWN
Regulation afternoon dress (black)
Cane and monocle—spats

DESCHAMPS
Regulation afternoon dress (black)
Cane—spats

GOURETTE
Street suit—vest—dark green tweed
White shirt—black tie and shoes

EDOUARD
Street suit, vest—light green and brown checks
Striped shirt—blue tie
Brown derby—black shoes—grey spats

HAIRDRESSER
Small black mustache
Black jacket—striped pants
White shirt—black tie—black shoes

CHIROPODIST
Long grey smock
Black pants—blue shirt—black tie and shoes

MANICURIST
Dark green dress—black apron
Black shoes

ACT I—SCENE II

COLOMBE
Street dress—dark pink
Matching shoes

MME. ALEXANDRA
Street dress—black
Large black hat
Black boa—black shoes
Parasol—costume jewelry

GOURETTE
Same as Act I, Scene I

POET-MINE-OWN
Same as Act I, Scene I

DESCHAMPS
Same as Act I, Scene I

MME. GEORGES
Same as Act I, Scene I

EDOUARD
Street suit—same as Act I, Scene I
Yellow vest—red tie

GAULOIS
Street suit—light tan
Homburg—light tan
Shoes—black patent leather—spats
Yellow cravat
Cane

ACT II, SCENE I

COLOMBE
(1st costume)

Street suit—walnut
Hat—walnut
Gloves and muff—walnut
Brown shoes

(2nd costume)

White petticoat
White camosole corset
Pale blue shoes

MME. ALEXANDRA
(1st costume)

Same as Act I, Scene I

(2nd costume)

White marchale costume (18th Century)
White hat
Yellow wig
White and gold baton

JULIEN
Regulation Army uniform (private)
(Underdress—Epilogue costume)

GAULOIS
Robe and slippers
Corset

POET-MINE-OWN
Same as Act I, Scene I

DESCHAMPS
Same as Act I, Scene I

CHIROPODIST
MME. GEORGES
HAIRDRESSER
MANICURIST
Same as Act I, Scene I

EDOUARD
Street suit—maroon

Yellow tie—striped shirt
Straw hat

GIRL
18th Century costume—white wig

BOY
18th Century costume—white wig

GOURETTE
(1st costume)

Same as Act I, Scene I

(2nd costume)

Marshal's costume—18th Century
No jacket and sword

ACT II—SCENE II

COLOMBE
Green costume and hat (18th Century)
Black shoes

JULIEN
Army uniform—Same as Act II, Scene I

MME. ALEXANDRA
(1st costume)

Same as Act II, Scene I

(2nd costume)

Dark red full-length cape—black shoes
Green lace head shawl—maroon gloves
Underdress (Epilogue costume)

GAULOIS
Maroon and gold costume (18th Century)
Brown wig—sword—black hat

GOURETTE
Marshal's costume (18th Century)
White wig—sword
Black hat with white plumes

MME. GEORGES
(1st costume)

Same as Act I, Scene I

(2nd costume)

Black cape—black hat

BOY *and* GIRL
Same as Act II, Scene I

1ST STAGEHAND
Light blue dungaree jacket and pants
Black beret—blue shirt—no collar
Red cummerbund—dark blue canvas shoes

2ND STAGEHAND
Black pants—brown vest
Striped shirt—no collar
Black shoes—large mustache

EPILOGUE

JULIEN
Black pants—cream shirt—no collar
Black shoes

COLOMBE
Street dress—light lavender
Black canvas shoes

MME. ALEXANDRA
Street dress—cream and grey
Large brown hat and gloves
Cream boa—black shoes—cane

GOURETTE
Same as Act I, Scene I
Dark brown topcoat and black derby

POET-MINE-OWN
Afternoon dress (light grey)

DESCHAMPS
Afternoon dress (light grey)

EDOUARD
Street suit—dark brown
Dark brown derby

MME. GEORGES
Dark striped skirt—black blouse
Red shawl

STAGEHANDS
Same as Act II, Scene II

MADEMOISELLE COLOMBE

SOUND EQUIPMENT

2 tape machines and mixer
2 amplifiers
2 large speakers (1 up Center) (1 down Right)

SOUND CUES

ACT II—SCENE I

Colombe's Dressing Room
CUE: 1 (As Gourette follows Alexandra off, calling:
        "On stage for Act One")
        Orchestra tuning up—(15 seconds) Up Cen-
        ter. Speaker
CUE: 2 (Right after tuning)
        3 taps on stage floor—manual—and immedi-
        ately following:
CUE: 3 Overture: ("Phedre"—massenet) 45 seconds
        —Up Center. Speaker
CUE: 4 (As Edouord enters Colombe's room)
        Fade overture—slowly

ACT II—SCENE II

Stage, "The Realm of Passion"
(Play-within-the-play)
CUE: 5 (Gaulois) ("I thank you on my knees)
        Trumpet—fan-fare (5 seconds) down Right.
        Speaker
CUE: 6 (As Gaulois exits)
        Trumpet—fan-fare (5 seconds) down Right.
        Speaker

CUE: 7 (Alexandra: "To make love bide the mor-
        row")
        Minuet (Mozart) (25 seconds) down Right.
        Speaker
CUE: 8 (Alexandra: "And swooning in each other's
        arms, forget love's woes")
        Segue: To: applause (45 seconds) down
        Right. Speaker
CUE: 9 (After 4 "little curtain" calls) (play-within-
        play)
        Fade out applause
CUE: 10 (As Julien starts to play the piano):
        (As off-stage pianist can be used as indicated
        in the script or recording below)
        A tape recording of Colombe singing: "Love
        is Gone" (1 minute) Up Center. Speaker
CUE: 11 (As Julien re-enters):
        Fade out song:

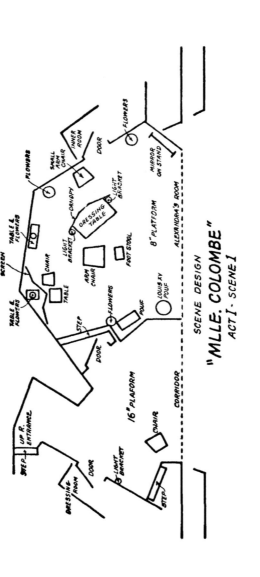

SCENE DESIGN
"MLLE. COLOMBE"
ACT I - SCENE I

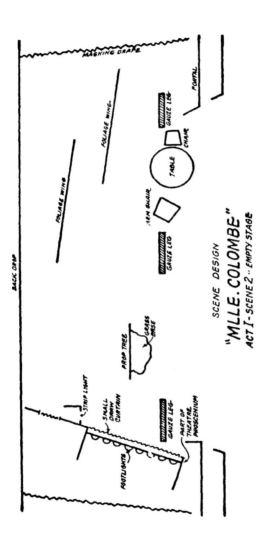

SCENE DESIGN
"MLLE. COLOMBE"
ACT I - SCENE 2 - EMPTY STAGE

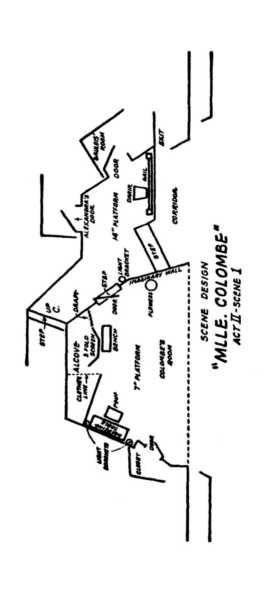

SCENE DESIGN
"MLLE. COLOMBE"
ACT II – SCENE I

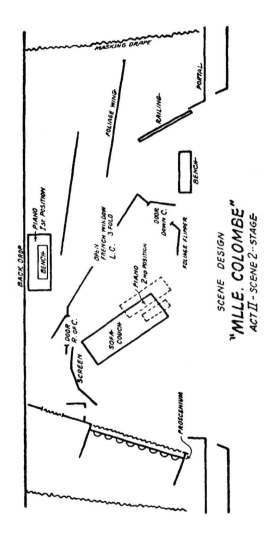

SCENE DESIGN

"MLLE. COLOMBE"

ACT II - SCENE 2 - STAGE

OTHER TITLES AVAILABLE FROM SAMUEL FRENCH

CAPTIVE
Jan Buttram

Comedy / 2m, 1f / Interior

A hilarious take on a father/daughter relationship, this off beat comedy combines foreign intrigue with down home philosophy. Sally Pound flees a bad marriage in New York and arrives at her parent's home in Texas hoping to borrow money from her brother to pay a debt to gangsters incurred by her husband. Her elderly parents are supposed to be vacationing in Israel, but she is greeted with a shotgun aimed by her irascible father who has been left home because of a minor car accident and is not at all happy to see her. When a news report indicates that Sally's mother may have been taken captive in the Middle East, Sally's hard-nosed brother insists that she keep father home until they receive definite word, and only then will he loan Sally the money. Sally fails to keep father in the dark, and he plans a rescue while she finds she is increasingly unable to skirt the painful truths of her life. The ornery father and his loveable but slightly-dysfunctional daughter come to a meeting of hearts and minds and solve both their problems.

TAKE HER, SHE'S MINE
Phoebe and Henry Ephron

Comedy / 11m, 6f / Various Sets

Art Carney and Phyllis Thaxter played the Broadway roles of parents of two typical American girls enroute to college. The story is based on the wild and wooly experiences the authors had with their daughters, Nora Ephron and Delia Ephron, themselves now well known writers. The phases of a girl's life are cause for enjoyment except to fearful fathers. Through the first two years, the authors tell us, college girls are frightfully sophisticated about all departments of human life. Then they pass into the "liberal" period of causes and humanitarianism, and some into the intellectual lethargy of beatniksville. Finally, they start to think seriously of their lives as grown ups. It's an experience in growing up, as much for the parents as for the girls.

"A warming comedy. A delightful play about parents vs kids. It's loaded with laughs. It's going to be a smash hit."
– *New York Mirror*

MURDER AMONG FRIENDS
Bob Barry

Comedy Thriller / 4m, 2f / Interior

Take an aging, exceedingly vain actor; his very rich wife; a double dealing, double loving agent, plunk them down in an elegant New York duplex and add dialogue crackling with wit and laughs, and you have the basic elements for an evening of pure, sophisticated entertainment. Angela, the wife and Ted, the agent, are lovers and plan to murder Palmer, the actor, during a contrived robbery on New Year's Eve. But actor and agent are also lovers and have an identical plan to do in the wife. A murder occurs, but not one of the planned ones.

"Clever, amusing, and very surprising."
– New York Times

"A slick, sophisticated show that is modern and very funny."
– WABC TV